Sublimity's Treasure
A Tale of Peculiar Findings, Discovery, & Hope

Michael Holbrook

Greetings!

I'm a ravenous reader and always have a book or two on hand. I had accumulated years of stubborn determination and horse sense by the time I began writing my books. Knowledge I may not have gained nor taken to heart had I elected to live life the other way around. I write from experience. Books give it a name, life makes it real.

Sublimity's Treasure is dedicated to all those who relish the discovery of new characters and unique settings. This is for book lovers everywhere.

Michael

The Desk

It is a simple, sturdy, wooden desk. A middle drawer dotted with ink from pens long since given up; the top etched with small, meandering lines from pencils and pen nibs complementing the random dimple from who knows what. The scattered mug stains are mostly on the upper left hand side, leading me to believe a previous owner was a lefty. The requisite colony of cobwebs and dust bunnies blanket the underside. On a whim, I paid fifteen bucks "as is, where is" at a cluttered yard sale in Sublimity, Oregon.

Nestled just north of Highway 22, seventeen miles east of the state capital city of Salem and a couple of leisurely driving hours west of Bend, Sublimity is a beautiful little bourgeois town of about 2,700 proud Pacific Northwesterners. An idyllic place with well-manicured spongy lawns neatly laid out side by side. Weed killers are either sold in warehouse-size containers or likely, not at all. Weeds wouldn't dare encroach on a Sublimity lawn. Driving through town, you almost expect to see Sheriff Taylor and Floyd, sitting on their bench outside the barber shop, enjoying the afternoon paper and gossiping about the locals. Sublimity is where Portland goes to kick off its shoes.

The desk made it home to Keizer where I unloaded it into our already cluttered two-car garage. I had to shuffle and restack some boxes and move some assorted odds and ends, but I squeezed it in. Amanda, my wife, had been on me to make room for vehicles and I knew this latest addition would not go unnoticed.

The Northwest climate had taken its toll on the desk. The drawers were a touch warped, hard to open, and didn't quite close as they might have in a earlier life, leaving a small, angled crack where they were once flush with the frame. In the large, lower right-hand drawer there were assorted sports pages touting the upcoming opener of the 1969 Seattle Pilots baseball team (their only year in Seattle before relocating to Milwaukee and becoming the Brewers), a couple of *Sports Illustrated* magazines—one featuring Chicago Cubs third baseman Ron Santo and another with a green and yellow clad Reggie Jackson then of the Oakland A's taking a mighty swing.

Beyond the desk's musty smell, and among the newspaper clippings and magazines, was a small leather journal. A utility-sized 6" X 9" specimen with a worn brown leather cover, filled with sixty-some stained and grease-smudged pages. I skimmed through, finding random pencil and pen scribbled notes, lists, and numbers, then flipped it, along with a few assorted paperclips and rusty staples, into the trash can. I picked up the magazines and took them into the kitchen to see what I had, figuring I might recoup the fifteen bucks selling them off to sports collectors. Worse to worst, I'd clip the best photos and frame them for the walls of my office or (still imaginary) man cave.

~

On my way to the kitchen, I passed Amanda in the utility room on her way out to the garage. I knew there was a round of tense conversation on the horizon when I heard her rustling about. I was in the kitchen with only the utility room door separating us and had the feeling it wasn't going to be nearly enough of a partition. I could hear her scooting things around, talking quietly to herself (usually a good sign) and every now and then mysteriously quiet (not always a good sign).

Grabbing a beer from the fridge, I tucked the old magazines under my arm and headed down the hall to my office. Closing the door behind me, I nudged my laptop to life and checked the day's baseball stats, poked around the Chicago Cubs page, Bryant and Rizzo's feats for the day, then took a peek at King Felix and the rest of the Seattle Mariners' numbers. My eyes were focused on the screen, but my ears were tuned towards the hallway. At any minute I was expecting the door to swing open and I'd have to explain how adding an antiquated desk would help make room for cars, much less my truck, which I figured would be indefinitely relegated to the driveway.

I had my argument polished and ready to go. I would tell her that I was going to refinish the desk and finally get rid of the worn metal boat-sized desk I'd purchased from Boeing surplus many years ago. I'd remind her that it would be a desk I would be proud to own and would relish the time I would take to lovingly restore it to its former beauty. Boom. I was ready.

I heard the utility door open and shut. Not a sound, not a peep, not a word.

Problem.

Putting the beer down, I quietly edged into the kitchen. She was reading something and didn't look up or acknowledge me. Thinking she found an old book in the garage, I was hoping to wiggle off the hook.

Nope.

Amanda leaned on the far end of the kitchen counter, seeming to struggle with her words before asking, "Who is—and I quote, 'that asshole Jimmy', and why do you owe him, and again I quote, '417 dollars'?"

"What are you talking about?" I asked, blindsided.

"What am I talking about? Well, let's revisit. Who is 'that asshole Jimmy' and why do you owe him four hundred seventeen dollars? Pretty straight forward isn't it, Christopher?"

She used my full first name—never a good sign. I was between a rock and a hard spot. I assured Amanda that although I knew plenty of assholes, not a one was named Jimmy. The questions then came in a flurry.

"How about Burnt Dog or Roully, or Bert, or—"

I held up my hands, palms out.

"Seriously, Amanda, if you are pissed off about something, just tell me." I was balancing between happy about not having to explain the addition in the garage and confused about the whole conversation. "What's this all about?"

"How about 'cigars—wanted whiskey. Will not trade.'?"

Amanda was upset—that much was obvious. But she may as well have been speaking in tongues. I had no clue what she was talking about. Before I could get a word in edgewise, she brought it to a head by tossing the journal on the countertop and demanding that I explain myself. It took a second before I realized it was the one I'd found in the desk and tossed just minutes earlier. She'd seen it, pulled it from the trash, and was flipping pages at a rapid pace. On the bright side, I figured I was a step ahead if I only had to explain the journal and not the desk.

I told Amanda where the journal came from, but didn't let well enough alone. I had to ask why she was going through the trash in the garage. I received a large helping about neatness and organization and her amazement that anything I touch even made it into the trash. I was surprised when she still didn't bring up the desk.

"You don't throw things away, you create mini-stacks of crap." She picked up a tattered, dusty Seattle Mariners media guide from the end table next to my recliner, leaving its outline on the table.

"Let it be," I said, grabbing for the book. "I'll put it away when I'm finished with it."

"Oh please," she said, clutching it in her left hand while running her right index finger along the edge. "You'll put it away when you're finished with it, huh? You haven't touched this thing in ages. See this dust? You know what that means?"

I chimed in before she could continue. "Yes, it means you need to dust more often." That no sooner left my mouth than I was mentally trying to reel it back in like a deep-sea fisherman fighting a Marlin. Nothing good could come from this, and after years of lessons I should know better.

She stared at me … through me … before turning her attention back to the journal. "I guess I should have known this wasn't yours," she said, sliding the notebook across the kitchen counter.

"How so?"

"Well, for starters," thumbing the fingers of her left hand, "there are references to cigars, bars, poker games—"

"Hey! I like that stuff, you know."

"Of course you do, sweetie," eyes rolled towards the ceiling, preparing to impose a penance as only she could. "Was my big man out last night smoking stogies, pounding whiskey, and raking in a big fat pot at Texas Hold 'em?" All this while scratching my chin like I were a puppy. "Did him have fun?"

Shaking off her hand and her sarcasm, I picked up the journal and flipped through a couple of pages. Sure enough, it appeared to be random "did/to do/don't do/must do/must avoid," lists written by a shaky hand. I grabbed the journal and my pride and moped my way back out to the garage. Sitting on the edge of my newly-acquired desk, I began reading in earnest.

Definitely not a diary. It told a story a day or a week at a time. Sometimes the entries were undated, other times months passed between scribbles. Most were run-of-the-mill life stuff. There were sports scores and stats (some more than a decade old), super bowl odds, assorted pages filled with numbers of additions and subtractions, grocery lists (Which I found odd—who keeps their old grocery lists? In fact, who writes their grocery needs in a journal?), a few names and phone numbers with single digit prefixes, random doodles, and margin notes. Individually, nothing of significance. In total, a knot-hole glimpse into someone's life.

"Why don't you find out who it belongs to?" Amanda startled me, having walked in to the garage while I was buried in the pages.

"Well, for one, I feel guilty going through someone else's papers."

"Would it be worse not to return it?""

"Ama, the magazines that were stacked in there with this thing … some are pretty old," I said. "This person could be long gone for all I know."

"But," she said, raising her right index finger, "Maybe not. Or, it might be important to a child or grandchild. Someone might really want this."

Knowing this wouldn't be the last of it, and thankful that she was coming round, I promised to swing out to Sublimity in the next few days and talk with the folks who'd sold the desk to me. As far as I was concerned, it would be a waste of time, forty mile, pain-in-the-ass drive. The way I saw it, she should have been happy that I managed to hit the trash can with it.

She spun and headed back into the house. As she did, she said over her shoulder, "We need to talk about that desk."

~

The following morning, Amanda came into the kitchen as I was sipping coffee and hovering over the journal. "Coffee's fresh and I put out a mug for you," I said, hoping to stave off an early morning desk conversation.

"Fascinated with your wild stranger, I see," she said, peering over my shoulder as she headed for the creamer.

"It's a whole other life, for sure. Look at this," I said, pointing at a passage and sliding the journal towards her.

Salem. Wants fifty by Thursday. Nate owes me. Meet at Bert's Tavern—he can pay.

"Fifty ... what?"

I shrugged. "I dunno."

"Well, it's your desk, it's your journal. Ask when you take it back out to Sublimity. Maybe you'll find some he-man answers," she said with a smirk that only a woman can give a man and get away with.

"You know, you're the one that wants me to take it out there. Why? What's the big deal? I finally hit the trashcan and you go digging it out."

No response.

"Tell you what. Next time I'm in Salem, I'll look for Bert's Tavern, okay? I'll just swing in there and ask. Besides, I might find my 'inner wildman'."

She gave me one last stare, turned away and said, "Knock yourself out, Tarzan."

~

If opposites attract, Amanda Chandler and I are a match made in heaven. While she is always on the go, always alert, always expecting an emergency, I'm more pragmatic, laid back, and considerably more sarcastic and dry of wit and humor. If I see two dogs having sex, I'll likely point and say, "Look, they're doing it doggy style!" Amanda, on the other hand, will pretend it isn't happening and that my mouth isn't moving. When we married, I told her if she takes my last name she would become Amanda Chandler Handler. This cracked me up to no end. Her, not so much.

The first time I put my knee to the floor and asked, "Amanda, will you marry me?" she replied, "Not in the least bit." It not only caught me off-guard, I wasn't sure if it was a no, a purposefully silly answer, or if she had just broken up with me. It was a confusing moment to say the least. It wasn't until a few years later, she confessed to hearing the line in an old movie and couldn't wait to use it on me. She said she'd wanted to say yes right away, but simply couldn't pass up the opportunity to make me wait, *and* to use the old film line. I eventually wore her down, and, with her having no real affinity for her maiden name, I was proud and honored to have Amanda as my beautiful bride.

Ama is a 5' 3" bundle of dynamite. I think she believes she has something to prove. To the world? Her dad? Herself? I'm never really sure. At eleven, she lost her mom to cancer. Her dad went AWOL shortly after. A good man she says, ever defending him, but not around much. She said he was less interested in filling family obligations than filling social voids. Amanda said he sobbed for days at the passing of her mom, his partner, his bride. She thinks it just took the life out of him. He drifted away, and Amanda and her father haven't spoken with each other in years. We've talked about it a few times, but not comfortably.

She was raised by her Mom's sister, whom Amanda called Auntie. Nothing more, just Auntie. As though hearing a starter pistol, Amanda bolted at eighteen, determined to be someone; to make something of her life. Her drive is a double edge sword. A loving wife. Focused. A taskmaster at times.

Amanda is a good person. I begrudge her nothing. When I met her, she'd worked for everything she had. She has earned, and wholeheartedly deserves, my respect.

Bert's Tavern

I headed out around 10:30 a.m., letting Amanda know I had a few errands to run. My errands took me directly in search of Bert's Tavern—if it indeed was still around. And, like most small neighborhood haunts, it was there, and probably would be until grandkids rechristen it something more timely, like *Ethan's* or *Jacob's*.

Bert's was a dimly-lit place that smelled of day-old beer and urinal cakes, like many other bars of similar ilk. Sandwiched between a bus stop and Alvareza's, a walk-up Mexican takeout joint, Bert's was both hard to find and hard to avoid. In 2009, the state of Oregon made bars healthier by banning indoor smoking, leaving sidewalks filled with jettisoned nicotine butts and forcing pedestrians (who were all too happy to steer clear) to navigate the curb around scorched, crushed, and often still smoldering cigarette debris and avoid becoming part of the smokers' huddle. To their credit, someone from Bert's had placed a three feet tall, neon green cigarette butt container and ashtray combo near the end of the block, close to the bus stop. I don't know if they were trying to be good Samaritans, getting paid by the city, or just looking to avoid problems, but it stood out like a landlocked lighthouse beacon to those smokers in the vicinity who took the time to use it.

I cruised in to Alvareza's for a burrito and discovered it to be nothing more than a satellite for travelers heading for Bert's. Bar regulars seemed to have made a habit of picking up a butt-burner or two and toting it back to their usual seat at the tavern next door. I aped the regulars and carried my lunch over to Bert's just a little before eleven. There was already a fistful of patrons—most of whom appeared as though they'd arrived that morning with Bert.

Feeling like a fish out of water, I ordered a beer and tried to blend in. This came with its own challenges. The guy behind the bar asked me if I wanted a draft. I wasn't sure, so I asked what they had. This didn't take long. The usual Super Bowl commercial brands and a couple local brews that helped anchor the place to the neighborhood. I asked for a lite and was told they didn't have that on tap. So I gave the best 'I'm a local' shrug that I could muster and asked for whatever was would go with my burrito. I got something with a few numbers and a lot of letters. An IPA and a seven or five on the intricately-detailed label. The brew was dark, and it was strong. My face did an involuntary mini-twitch. Trying to be cool, I checked out the room and nodded to the music. At pre-noon there was no problem with a bit of Sinatra.

I asked who ran the place and the bartender said that he did. I asked who the place was named for and he replied that it was named after him. He seemed to be getting a chuckle out of my ignorance so I just asked him, "Are you Bert as in 'Bert's Tavern'?"

"In the flesh," he said, reaching across the bar to shake my hand. "Welcome. You must be new around here," he added with a smile, "I always like fresh blood."

I told him that I didn't often visit the area and he asked, "Married?"

"Yes, but that's not why I haven't been around," I said trying to think of a better answer and coming up empty. I got right to the point. "I found this in an old desk I bought in Sublimity a short time back, and I'd like to find its owner."

I reached into my courier bag, fished out the journal, and dropped it on the bar top. "It has a few references to this place and I thought you might be able to help." He flipped through a couple pages with a short, wrinkled smile creeping onto his face every now and again. At length, he closed it and pushed it back towards me.

"That thing belongs to Hore."

"Huh?"

"Yeah, the son-of-a-gun still has an open bar tab. I usually let it go because he had some of the Goddamnest stories you ever heard. Sometimes I felt as though I should be paying him."

"I mean, 'Hore'? That's his name?"

"Oh, that," he said with a chuckle. "Well, Hore told me a story about growing up in some hick town in the Midwest. Said they didn't have much. As a kid, he said they'd take car rides to the nearest burg and they'd drive through these streets lined with brick houses and shaved lawns, dotted with massive shade trees of oak, maple, elm, and sycamore. Told how laying up in the rear window of the car he felt like a bug traveling through giant stalks of broccoli."

"What does that have to do with calling him Hore?"

"I asked him the same thing. He just kept on talking about broccoli. Told me that's why he won't eat it. Said it's probably covered with squirrel and crow shit. Said you can't just rinse it off and have anything worth putting into your face."

I shook my head. It was beginning to feel like we were having separate conversations. But, I bit. "Where was this?"

"I haven't asked, he hasn't said. He liked to talk and seemed to enjoy that I pretended to listen. Like you, I guess," he added, wiping at the bar. "Oh, and by the way, I believe that was his name. Hore."

He got me on that, reeled me in nice and slow.

"So, does ... um ... *Hore* come in often? And Christ, that's really his name?"

"This is a bar, my friend. If someone tells me his name is Santa Claus, that's good enough for me. By closing time this place is filled with Elvis pretenders and Kung Fu experts."

"Does he come in regularly?"

"He's random. Sometimes every few days, then I won't see him for weeks. I can set my watch to most of the people that come in. Not him."

"Who does he come in with?"

"No one I remember. Just comes in, reads a paper, has a couple drinks."

"Well, the reason I'm asking is because, in here," I said tapping on the journal, "there's a page with a note about bringing money to Bert's."

"Well, how about that. Last time he was here, the old prick spent most of the day and then strolled out. Stiffed me. Didn't figure I'd see him again. Wouldn't have hurt, but he was here a good long while."

"When was this?"

"Three, maybe four months back. I'd given up on him."

"How much?"

"Four bucks."

"He sat here for most of a day and milked a four dollar tab?"

He chuckled, his heavy torso moving along with his wispy hair. "Oh, shit. No, no. I thought you were asking how much *you* owed. I'd have to check, but close as I can recall, forty-five, fifty bucks."

"That's a lot of beer."

"Yeah, he didn't seem to be in any hurry." After a quick pause, he said, "I didn't cut him off because he seemed okay. You know, just relaxed."

"Was that normal?"

"Yeah, he was always laid back, never in any kind of hurry."

"No, I mean drinking nine or ten beers." I was getting flustered with our conversation.

"Oh, no. That was unusual—aside from stiffing me. Typically he'd have a couple, drop a ten on the bar, fold his paper, and leave."

I thanked Bert, then sat there for a while spinning my glass between my palms, thinking about this 'Hore' fellow. *Why the hell do I care? Why should I?* God help me, but I do love a good mystery. I've read hundreds through the years but that was as far as it went. Until now. Now I felt like I had a case of my own. A mystery to solve for an inquisitive client—me.

I pulled thirty bucks from my wallet and dropped ten of it on the bar. I scribbled my name and cell number on a napkin and neatly folded it, the twenty snuggly tucked inside. Bert was shooting the breeze with a few guys near the door and I handed it to him on my way out. "If the guy comes back in, have him give me a call," I said, and stepped outside, shading my eyes and blinking as I adjusted to the sunshine. Walking to my truck and looking around, feeling a cozy Pacific breeze wash over me, I made the executive decision that it was just too nice of a day to head back home.

Back to Sublimity

I reckoned as long as I was in Salem, I'd take a quick jaunt east to Sublimity. After having mulled it over the past few days, I'd become fixated with that old journal. While my head tells me to throw it in the trash and forget about it, my gut tells me to have some fun with it. Amanda would probably say that's part of my Walter Mitty makeup. That I'm never satisfied with where I am or what I'm doing, always assuming there is untold mystery, mayhem, and intrigue in everyone else's life and on all the other streets and blocks and towns were we don't live. I smiled, arm out the open window, elbow on the window ledge. She's right. I dream. Then again, she was the one who called me Tarzan.

Cruising east along Route 22, I thought about what I was going to say. I mean, "Hi. You sold a desk to me and I want to know who the junk inside belongs to," isn't really a gold-standard opening line. Or worse, "I found a journal and I'm on a hunt for the owner." I laughed to myself, thinking, *maybe I should be wearing a trench coat.* Then I realized none of this is funny if they are private people who don't appreciate strangers.

Pulling into Sublmity, I couldn't help but notice that the street, the entire town—as usual—was quiet. Too quiet. And neat. Too neat. I realized I wouldn't last a minute here. I'd have to throw something in my front yard—a kid's pool, an old chair, a rusty BBQ grill—something, *anything*, just to make a point. I located the house, pulled into the driveway, and climbed out of my trusty Ford pick-up—fading red paint standing out like a sore thumb—and headed for the door. Now, I'm terrified of dogs, but had no fear of one leaping out at me snarling, gritting its teeth, fangs exposed, and slobber dripping off its muzzle. Not here. I question if dogs are allowed to bark and doubt it would be tolerated. I opened the screen and gave the green wooden door a quick shave and a haircut.

A woman wearing a bright sundress answered. I recognized her as the person who'd sold the desk to me. We had the usual, 'Who are you, what do you want, sorry to bother you, I promise I'm not selling anything,' eyeball exchange and I introduced myself. She said her name was Petula and, after a few cobwebs collapsed, she recalled me (or was nice enough to pretend as much). She jumped to say that all sales were final. I assured her I was pleased with the desk.

"I found a journal in one of the drawers and would like to get it back to its rightful owner."

She looked towards her eyebrows for a few seconds, crossed her arms and said, "I'm sorry, I really can't help. My partner and I just bought this place a short time ago and that desk—your desk—was one of the things clogging the garage. It's one of the reasons we had the sale. There was a ton of things stuffed in the shed, and the garage had crap all over the place. Whoever lived here didn't give much thought for anyone else before they bailed."

"Can you tell me the seller's name?"

She shrugged and said, "We bought through an agent. Never met the seller."

I knew that not having much buyer/seller contact, save the incidental meetings during the usual appraisals, inspections, and good faith stuff, was typical, especially so when a house was unoccupied and on the selling block.

"Can you give me the agent's name? I'll just give them a call and won't trouble you any further."

She asked me to wait, didn't invite me in, and disappeared behind the screen mesh. After a long minute she returned, extending a business card.

"This is who we worked with."

I took the card, offered thanks, and returned to my truck. After sliding in and buckling up, I sat for a moment tapping the card and giving thought to this whole thing. Here I am, sitting in a stranger's driveway, in the middle of a silent community, and for what? I twisted the key, fired up the engine, tugged into reverse, and, without looking, backed out of the driveway. Surprise. Not a car or horn honking within miles.

On my way home I put the phone on speaker and called Amanda. Voicemail. That meant one of a couple things. She was busy, she was in the garden, or she was pissed. A three-sided coin toss. I left a message, "Home in a half hour, can I pick up anything from the store?" Penance paid, my mind drifted. I was wrestling with the big picture. *Why do I care about a stranger's journal? Why does any of this even matter?* Easy answer—it doesn't. No one gives a rip. It's just an old journal in an old desk. And, perhaps that's why *I* care.

I made a mental note to call the real estate agent on Monday after Amanda headed out to work. I'm not much of a Sam Spade and I don't expect to stumble across the Maltese Falcon, but this journal was the closest thing I've had to a hobby in a long while.

Home Sweet Home

"*Home Sweet Home.*" That's what the hand-painted wood plaque over the mudroom door reads. All curly lettering surrounded by vines and happy little birds. I reached up, gave it three quick, quiet taps and strolled into the kitchen.

Amanda was in the living room poring over a textbook. I could tell she was waiting for me to interrupt, for no other reason than to accuse me of interrupting. I'm probably wrong about that, but at times, that's sure how it feels. Before I could say anything though, she asked, "Did you get the stuff from the store?" Didn't look up.

Oh shit.

"I called and asked if you wanted anything."

"And I sent you a text. Don't you check for answers when you ask questions?"

I wanted to tell her that I *called* her and she could have done the same and I'd have gotten the message and gone to the store. My Spidey senses told me better and for once my common-sense neurons connected before I opened my mouth and started moving my lips. I instead said, "I'm sorry, babe. I was driving and didn't hear the chime, plus I can't really text and drive at the same time. I would be happy to go to the store now."

She looked straight up at me. "But you can talk on the phone and drive?"

~

Just after turning thirty-two, Amanda enrolled at an online college to pursue a master's degree, and I've walked on eggshells since. Even though I work from home as a newspaper columnist, I am still getting used to maintaining silence after 6 p.m. She comes home, we eat for fifteen minutes, pretend to have a bunch of new stuff to say to each other, and then she disappears into her books or online class session. At which point the TV, stereo, phones, or other noises are not in my best interest.

"So, what errands did you do?"

Ah, shit.

Think fast, Sparky. "We've had that broken slat along the west side of the backyard fence since one of the neighborhood kids managed to break it off. I figured I'd cruise over to the lumberyard to see if I could find a matching replacement. No luck."

Hoping to end the conversation, I quickly walked back into the kitchen. Sure, I felt bad lying like that, but have learned from experience not to piss in the bath water. I was tired. It wasn't the beer. I wasn't sure what it was. Certainly wasn't my job either. I'd been writing a thrice-weekly sports column for the daily going on eight years. It was to the point where I could grind out decent, readable copy in less than a day. Mind you, my readers are not stupid, but let's face it: "Tucking the football and angling for the end zone for the game-winning touchdown," is more readable than, "The old chap firmly grasped the dimpled pigskin and scampered gracefully for the score."

Anyway, three columns, three (long) days of work, full time pay. At first it was a great feeling. All my life I've liked nothing more than sports and talking about sports. I have a face made for radio as the saying goes, but not the voice for it. Thus, my *Chris is Crossed* column (which many refer to as "Chris is Pissed," as I take out a lot of life's frustrations on those sports multi-millionaires). Often self-entitled, often egomaniacs, and surprisingly often, decent, honest, down-to-earth people. The former pay the bills, the later make it possible.

My gig provides some flextime, and a side-project like this journal is just the distraction I need. So long as Amanda thinks I'm busy all day and the boss is happy with the facts and opinions I crank out every Tuesday, Thursday, and Sunday without having to concern herself with lawsuits, I stay under radar.

Sometimes, like now, I just want to relax, let go, and disappear. And that's one thing Amanda's new college ambitions are giving me. Time to disappear. I don't need to worry about Ama wanting to participate in sports with me. When we first got together I suggested a game of catch. She shrugged and we headed into the yard. I picked up a large sixteen inch softball and underhanded it to her. She turned sideways, raised her knee to her waist, her arms and hands to her face, and shrieked, "Stop throwing things at me!" I knew then, that sports were not her thing. (Though she did appear as if she were mimicking the Heisman Trophy stance. Something I kept to myself, lest I had to explain it.)

~

That evening, I sat in the back yard from about 8:20 p.m. until nearly 11:30 p.m. I read for a while, stared at nothing for a while, and thumbed through the journal for a while. It was hot for Oregon, record-breaking hot, and muggy to boot, with humidity at shirt-tugging levels. Earlier, the large plastic thermometer mounted on the covered edge of a patio beam had crept near the one-hundred degree mark. Not even a mosquito bothered with me. Silent.

I flipped through the journal as I had numerous times before. Some pages framed coffee or glass rim stains, some dog-eared, while others filled with no more than mindless doodles. Nothing that would cause a person to give it a second thought. Maybe it was those sports magazines in the desk drawer. Maybe I was just curious about a man who enjoyed sports. Curious about what, if anything, those specific notes and doodles meant to him. As a lifelong Cubs fan, maybe I was simply looking for a sympathetic shoulder to proverbially cry on.

A neighbor was running their back yard sprinkler, and I watched it appear and disappear over the fence. Silent, except for a lone plane overhead. Surely its props were beating only to cool the inhabitants. Even silent, I knew we were all here. Enduring the heat, windows wide open and unheard fans swirling. Ninety-five to a hundred degrees here is uncommon. People lay low, talk in small voices, and complain about the heat. Suburban silence at its most deafening. Only crickets, matching my heartbeat in rhythmic chirps. When they go silent it grows darker, like dimming a light little by little. Scares the shit out of me, because I know that something's always out there, somewhere. I don't know how rural folks do it. Or, perhaps, that explains their inevitable dogs. Loud, big, scary dogs. Not a fan.

~

I was in the garage sanding my new old desk when it occurred to me that this timeworn piece of furniture had become my personal worry stone. While working on it, I'd solved all the world's mysteries (well, in my head at least). The desk was showing the results of my contemplations. Free of paint and old stains, its tight oak grain breathed new life. I was excited about giving it a new finish yet found myself putting it off—not ready for the project to end. The desk wasn't done telling me stories that I need to hear or sharing lessons I needed to learn.

Eventually, a rich, deep stain would soak into the fine, hearty wood and provide a proud, striking surface. This meshed with my visions of sitting behind a manual typewriter—cigar or pipe at hand—cranking out the next great novel of our times. That I did not own a manual typewriter and only occasionally enjoyed a good cigar was beside the point. The desk was the best fifteen dollar investment I'd made in some time. Her bejeweled reflective finish would be the pinnacle. Not a museum piece, but all mine.

Sooner or later, I figured I'd solve all those old pencil-thin mustache mysteries. I'll be able to get rid of the dented, gray metal desk I bought from Boeing Surplus years ago. It was the first real desk I'd ever owned, right out of the University of Washington—ready to set the world ablaze. Seems like yesterday, but this yesterday was a memory more than twenty years old. That old desk has served me well, as it had (in my imagination) the creator and chief designer of Boeing's greatest jets.

My Grandfather told me stories about how Bill Boeing's boat company began manufacturing aircraft in World War II. A good move for Mr. Boeing. The eponymous company has survived numerous ups and downs, including the early 1970s 'Boeing Bust.' Boeing, at the time the Seattle region's largest employer, saw its payroll shrink from a peak of nearly 101,000 employees in 1967 to fewer than 39,000 by April 1971. Two local Realtors even purchased and placed a billboard near Seattle-Tacoma's International Airport reading: "Will the last person leaving

SEATTLE - <u>Turn out the lights</u>." Happily, Boeing's fortunes changed, they purchased new furniture, and I'm the proud owner of the desk on which the company's future president (again, in my imagination—don't ruin it for me) took off. But now I had this beautiful, wooden replacement. It will find its way into my office and Boeing will fly away at our next community yard sale. Seems the only mystery I hadn't solved was that journal. It had become quite the bee in my bonnet.

Real Estate

By Sunday evening the desk was ready for wood putty, a little touch-up, and some TLC. On Monday morning, I dug out the Realtor's card that Petula gave me and called the cell number listed. After four rings—voicemail. I left a message indicating that I had a question about a house, figuring that the truth was good but too much wasn't. I followed that up with a direct call to the real estate office and was told that Derick Thompson wasn't in. I thanked the person and hung up.

I was working on a column about Ichiro Suzuki's lasting legacy with the Seattle Mariners, mind wandering. *It's just an old journal in an old desk.* I finished my piece, expounding on Ichiro's already incredible achievements and hypothesizing what might have been had he played his entire career in America, when my phone began chiming out *Good Vibrations.*

Yes, Derrick Thompson was the selling agent on the Sublimity house. No, I wasn't looking to buy or sell. No, I wasn't looking for a comparative market analysis. Yes, I know that online estimates can be way off mark. Yes, Sublimity is a beautiful place. After three rounds of sparring, I jumped in when Mr. Thompson paused to make sure he hadn't missed an angle. Before he could extend his pitch about vacation and rental properties, I asked if he could tell me the seller's name.

"It was listed through an attorney, which I always hate, because attorneys make things so much more complicated." After he rushed an apology, I assured him I wasn't an attorney and asked if he could provide the listing agent's name and number. He did, with the closing plea that I let Ms. Rasmussen know that I already have an agent (him), and to let him know when I was ready to depart with or acquire real property.

If Amanda followed routine, she'd be home from work in about an hour. I figured now was the best time to call. Sarah Rasmussen answered on the second ring. I did the dance of explaining who I was and what I was looking for. Ms. Rasmussen was professional and cut right to the chase. She informed me that she wasn't at liberty to provide information and that my best bet would be to go through the county's public records. It wasn't what I wanted to hear, but I thanked her and ended the call, again second guessing myself on why and if it mattered.

The Home Front

Amanda was rubbing the back of her neck and wasted no time heading down the hall to our bedroom when she got home from work. I could see on her face that it could be a bumpy evening, so I thought I'd offer to take her out to dinner. I waited a few seconds then followed her to our bedroom. Before I could suggest dinner, she had already torn off her work outfit and was slipping into comfy clothes. I got as far as, "We should go to—" before she nailed me.

With her eyes narrowing, she softly, but firmly, cut me off. "No. If *we* should go *anywhere*, *you're* driving, in *your* truck, by *yourself.*" Not exactly what I was hoping to hear. Her touchiness told me all I needed to know about her day. Looked like a pizza night.

We did share pizza and a sensibly-priced bottle of Willamette Valley Pinot Noir. She eventually allowed herself to relax and told me about her day: a run-in with the copier repair person, problems with freight shippers, and uncooperative coworkers. She went off on her semi-usual speech of a regretted Art History degree and how she couldn't wait to have her Masters so she could tell her boss just where he could stick his office manager job. I wanted to remind her that she might be able to use the new degree at her present company, but deep down I knew better. She'd burned too many bridges in her haste to get away from her current role, and there wasn't enough lumber and materials in Oregon to rebuild it. I settled for, "My day went well. The Ichiro piece is put to bed." I was cognizant that she hadn't asked about my day, and gave me a look confirming her awareness of same.

Most people I know like to talk about their job, but Amanda is a sports fan only when I really, *really* urge her to join me a game (tickets are a perk) or watch one on the tube. We don't otherwise engage in much, "who's adjusting their cup, spitting on the field, swearing, doing weird end zone dances, driving the fastest car going left for three hours, or breaking records," chitchat. While this might be upsetting for some in my profession, it works well for us.

I should confess a couple of things. While Amanda can be a handful (I have a saying: "When my wife's happy, I'm happy. When she's not happy, I'm not allowed to be happy."), she isn't nearly as grumpy as I sometimes make her out to be.

Take a recent back-and-forth we had about … toilet tissue. It began with me stating the obvious: I was heading into the bathroom that she had just used, and the toilet paper roll was empty. I pointed this out (mistake) and was provided with an A-team debate squad version of how it couldn't be her lapse. She was speaking about logistics and probabilities, but what I heard was that I had apparently latched onto a conspiracy theory in which someone sneaks into our bathroom, uses all the toilet paper, leaves the empty roll, and then—like the Easter Bunny, Tooth Fairy, and Santa Claus—disappears. Yup. My fault. How dare I even consider questions while in the land of female logic? I'm never sure if it's tongue-in-cheek sarcasm or her way of apologizing.

Anyway, after din-din, Amanda settled in to work on cobbling together another rung on her office-manager escape plan and I headed back to my office. We owned a single story house, not huge, not small. 1,500 sq. ft. with three bedrooms and two baths. As we have no children, what that really means is we have a master bedroom, my office, and a guest room. For just the two of us, it seems much larger than it is. Amanda could easily do her homework in the guest room. She already has a rarely-used corner desk in there, and it would be easy to turn it into another office. Instead, she chooses to work at the dining room table. For me that's a plus, as my office is at the opposite end of the house. The downside? Our large, flat screen TV is situated just feet from the dining room.

I thought this would be a great time to get a jump on my next column so I powered up my laptop, opened a new document, and stared at the curser. I typed the due date as title, saved, and closed the file. Nothing even a hard-eyed, red-pen hearted editor could find wrong with that! Online, I searched, "finding property sellers." I refined the search to "Marion County Oregon Property Records," and eventually realized there was no magical online solution. I made a note to swing into the Marion County Clerk's offices in Salem and went back to work.

~

Amanda is not a morning person. Not only does she not form complete sentences before coffee, simple words themselves are often a struggle. A slew of er … gaaa … baaa … and grunts mingled with a gaggle of feigning, shrugging, and jutting gestures. That was typical morning conversation from 6:10 a.m. to 6:35 a.m. I once bought her a mug that was stenciled, "Unless you are reading the bottom of this mug, don't talk to me."

Mondays, like today, are especially difficult. When the noun and verb procession did begin, I grasped the blessing I'd overlooked in her silence just moments before. See, the pointing and jutting were annoying but not leaving powder burns. When she began forming words, it wasn't always lovey-dovey morning kissy-kissy stuff. She often managed to lob in an occasional four letter salvo, punctuated with finger thrusts.

I learned long ago not to reply, but to listen. I'm sure my eyes were set in the, "what the hell is wrong with you" stare, but there was no way it was going to come out of my mouth. Now upstairs, in my head, I was tearing her a new one. Upstairs, I was the king of oratorical kick-ass.

With caffeine's help, we manage to come down from our Mr. and Mrs. Hyde personas, return to usual marital conversation, and prepare to face the day— both thankful that it's Monday only once a week.

I could tell that Amanda had something on her mind and she could tell that I knew. (I often think marriage provides both partners powers of mental telepathy.) She cut straight to the crux. "This journal thing is weird, Chris. You hang out in bars, you talk with people you never acknowledged before, and you're gone. A lot. What am I supposed to think?"

"Well, let's see here," I said, and I began counting off the items on my fingers. "You're saying I'm independent, have friends, and found a hobby. Wow. Terrible, huh?" She turned away. "I know you are concerned and doing your best to tell me you love me, and that I'm on a wild goose chase, but, you know what, Amanda? I'm happy. This is good for me, and if it's good for me, in the long run, it's good for us."

I sensed she was feeling a loss of control. She seemed sad as much as anything. It wasn't as though she was lamenting that I spend every day sitting in a bar somewhere. But she can be a control freak, and, having experienced much loss and faced myriad challenges in her life, she likely felt out-of-sorts about the whole thing.

I reached across the small table and grasped her hands. Looking into her eyes I said, "Amanda, you will never have reason to question my love or devotion to you. To us. For us. I will never put that at risk." Letting go of her hands and putting my hands on the table, palms up, I said, "I'm just, well, enjoying the hell out of this. It has taken me out of my self-imposed comfort zone and it brings me a purpose. A goal. A challenge outside of writing about the Portland Trailblazers or Seattle Seahawks. It's my diversion. You—you are my life." We shared a warm hug, a sloppy morning coffee kiss, and left it at that.

Digging for Information

The Marion County Court Recorder's office is located, tellingly enough, on Court Street. I couldn't find what I was looking for online without forking over a credit card number and other personal info to some questionable site I'd never heard of. So, here I was, just a few blocks east of downtown Salem, our state capital, on a drizzly Monday morning.

It took no time at all to find a parking space, a pleasant surprise on a wet day—no jogging or speed walking necessary (for which my desk body is grateful). Rain dotted my jacket and shoes, ball cap saving my hair and glasses. Why no umbrella? Most old school Northwesterners are used to Pacific Graylight Time during fall, winter, and spring months and don't often carry or use an umbrella. That's how we separate locals from tourists. It's a stubborn trait that tells Mother Nature, "We love you and we appreciate the rain, but we won't let it affect our day-to-day life." I've heard Alaskans say the same thing about their weather but they use common sense and wear parkas and boots. I have noticed however, over the past decade or so, the younger web-footed offspring around here don't cling to the hardy lore of us 'elders,' and teens can be seen hovering around malls area-wide sprouting umbrellas and clinging to their cardboard coffee or tea containers. The times, they are-a-changing.

It took only a few minutes to navigate the signage and find what I was looking for, all the while thankful I wasn't attempting this in Portland or Seattle or San Francisco where I figured I'd lose half a day and develop an ulcer. I justified my little bit of Sherlockian antics by promising to pretend to work late this evening. After a short time I'd unraveled the mini-math and learned that the property seller, Celia Browne, had authorized someone named Anthony Jenkins, as agent, under Power of Attorney, to handle the transaction.

I knew that Mr. Jenkins wasn't necessarily an attorney, but judging by the way the real estate agents hadn't wanted any part of this, my money was on the lawyer horse. I scribbled down the relevant notes, bypassing the friendly clerk's offer to make copies for money. I don't recall the amount, but as soon as I learned it wasn't free, my brain turned off and, by habit, my reporter's notebook opened and my pen clicked to life.

Back in my truck, I sat and considered the options. Maybe Anthony Jenkins was Celia Browne's brother. Or husband. Or ex-husband. Maybe he was a pro-bono resource. Interesting side note: Pro-bono means, "for the public good." You can imagine that many lawyers don't enjoy pro-bono work. Then again, I suppose a ditch-digger, or a trash collector, or a house painter, or most of the rest of us aren't much for mandated pro-bono work either. Imagine being told you had to paint your neighbor's house for the "public good," (though many color schemes I see could stand a cover-up for the good of the public). Artists flock to it though. You know—provide their work for free to get their work seen and their name out, all in hopes of one day *not* doing pro-bono work. Interesting turn of the table. (Yes, I know, stay focused. I get that a lot.)

Whether Jenkins was Browne's brother, mother, sister, father, or lawyer didn't really much matter to me. In fact, I was struggling to figure out what *did* matter. My looming doubts were returning.

I checked my watch: 12:35 p.m. I had an afternoon ahead of me. A column to write. And a journal to forget about. By 1:00 p.m. I was ordering a beer, by name, from Bert, by name.

~

I'd futzed around with this journal to the point where Amanda's words from a recent filibuster on the topic were bouncing around in my head and beginning to make sense. "Take up stamp collecting or something," she said, with a wide-reaching arc of her arm. "This is just an old piece of trash you found in a desk at a garage sale. It's not a Mona Lisa. It's not Hemmingway's lost journal. It's just the ramblings of someone who was probably taking notes to remember who to collect from for mowing their lawn or cleaning their gutters." She had paused, seemingly lost for words, before finishing with a most reasonable question, "What is your deal?"

To be fair, I didn't have a plausible answer loaded in the chamber for her. But I did have one for me: Sure, it's just an old journal. Not even a diary. Just snippets of things done, places to go, errands to complete, and every now and again a short rambling about someone or something. Old and ragged and certainly doesn't hold the key to buried treasure in the Sierra Madres. But, it has taken on a life of its own. Page after page of a person's life. Someone *different*. Someone who took that other fork in the road, and I want to know more.

Bert suggested I chat with a guy named Roully. He gave the impression that Roully was the only person Hore spent much time with. Before I made a commitment about furthering my quest one way or the other, I determined that I would either talk with Hore or this Roully character, either of whom, Bert said, could be found hanging around his place—hit or miss. The only common denominator was a tavern. Probably not the best of origins and carrying a 99.9% certainty of being a thorn in my bride's side.

~

Wednesday morning, Amanda had a cold coming on hard and sent me to the store for facial tissue, cough drops, and minestrone soup. A three-item list I felt confident in successfully pulling off. She'd been sniffling around for a day or two but this morning it really hit her. Now, guys often get a bad rap for being babies when we get sick, but my dear wife can whine with the best of us. She starts the "woe is me," at the first hint of feeling ill and when the cold or flu really hits, she kicks it into over-whine. That said, I still give her credit. For me, going to the doctor was easier as a kid. He'd pinch my nuts, look in my ears, and tell me to go outside and play. Whole different story at my age. My last exam at the urologist was a typical example. Midway through what I believed was a lengthy prostate exam, the doctor said "you have a small prostate." I replied, "Then use your pinky."

Anyway, it was a quick trip to the store. I thought about running over to Target at Keizer Station but opted to stay near town and hit the local market instead. Boom. Forty-five minutes, round trip. Forgot nothing. New record! Of course Keizer isn't large, a little more than 37,000 people scattered over seven square miles, but snug against the state capital, so I still gave myself a mental high-five for my timing.

Ama was appreciative to have her (as she calls it) "feeling-like-shit kit." I felt for her as this was a busy week and she was stressed about her classes. However (yup) … the inner butthead in me thoroughly appreciated the quiet, along with the opportunities that were sure to follow. See, when she doesn't feel well, I'm like a kid on an unsupervised trek to the park. Not going to do anything stupid or rash, but enjoying the time to theoretically bark, yell, howl, scratch, burp, fart, and do so without so much as a glance over my shoulder. Now, don't get me wrong, I want my wife healthy and over her cold or flu or whatever bug had grabbed her, as quickly as possible. Just sometimes, in cases like this, I look at the clock and see Salvador Dali's *The Persistence of Memory*.

The better-half suitably nestled into the sofa, I headed to my office. It took about two hours to finish banging out my column on how I felt about the National Football League's concussion protocol (a code that I find lightweight, lip service, being pushed by outside parties, trying not to get sued while trying to appear concerned for affected players suffering game-related issues later in life, and not nearly comprehensive enough). I saved the document, figuring I'd review it later, add a couple more thoughts, and then push it to my editor. I love working remote.

Tiptoeing into the living room, I found Amanda napping on the sofa, book on her lap, and clicked the side-table lamp's three-way bulb down to low. Back in my office, I began reading through my notes about the journal, or "the book," as I'd often come to think of it. Not sure if I mentally meant that as a generic reference about the journal or if I was subtly telling myself that I was going to write about it. Either way, I had notes piling up that kept me interested. For now, that was enough.

Alex

With some free time on my hands, I gave my pal Alex a call to see if he'd like to meet for a beer. I've known Alex for more than ten years. He works for an online sports site and is Oscar Madison personified. I sometimes think I secretly live through him, and secretly, I think he lives through me as well, though neither of us will ever admit it.

Now, before I get too far into this, there are a few things you need to know about Alex. For instance, he is creative—but not always in the most adult sense. He once kept a late-night radio call-in host on the edge of his seat by spinning an incredible tale of alien abduction. The host was hanging onto every word surrounding his capture and subsequent probe at the hands of these strange creatures—all broadcast over local AM waves to a small, but captive and gullible audience. He was telling his story in great detail. Having his belt laser-beamed in half, clothes ripped apart, and being forcefully secured to a table, unable to move. After a few intense minutes, Alex took dramatic pause and said, "Well, I *think* I was being probed by a Martian. I'd been drinking since noon. It might have been a *Martin*. Things were kind of hazy," and then hung up the phone. Alex can be disgusting, but funny. I'm sure Amanda would give an entirely different perspective.

Anyhoo, you would have thought I'd called to tell him that Jesus had re-charged his batteries and resurrected.

"A beer? You? In the middle of the week? In the middle of the day?" he said, part cynical and part incredulous, until I interrupted his shtick.

"How about Bert's? You know where that is?" I was peeking into the front room making sure the boss was still asleep. No drool, but a few rumbling snorts. I figured I was safe. Alex assured me that he knew where the place was and we agreed to meet in thirty minutes.

To his point, it *was* an odd feeling. I felt like a high school kid sneaking out in the middle of the night to meet up with friends possessing similar cat burglar skills. Even back then though, we didn't do anything malicious. Three or four of us would gather around 2 a.m. and share a few misappropriated beers. We'd stand around, passing the can back and forth between us, complain about girls, scratch ourselves, and try to one-up each other. You know, basically the same things people ten years older were doing in bars.

Alex was hunched over the bar nursing a draft when I got there. "Well, I don't believe it. You really showed up. Impressive, Mr. C. Impressive." I waved off his comments and ordered one of whatever Alex was working on. I asked the barkeep if Bert was around. He replied that Bert had taken the afternoon off. Alex was stunned. "You mean to tell me that not only did you show up, but you *know* the guy this place is named for?"

It was my turn for a little fun.

"Yes, I do," I said, thanking the bartender for the beer. "Bert and I are friends, in fact." Alex, for one of the few times since I'd known him, said nothing—just stared at me. "What can I say? Bert and I are buds. You need to get out more," I said, with a self-gratifying grin.

Regaining his wit he said, "So, to what do I owe the pleasure?"

"Nothing special, big guy. I had some free time, and thought 'Hey, I should see if Alex is available!'"

"Bullshit."

"Seriously. Why can't a couple of guys meet up for a couple of beers?"

"Because I know your wife, remember?" He stared at the high-octane bottles lined up along the back of the bar for a few seconds before spinning around to face me, Cheshire grin at the ready. "She's out of town, isn't she?"

"For your information," I said, "She's not. She's at home, even as we speak."

"Son-of-a-bitch," he said. "Well then, here's to your nuts!" as he hoisted his beer.

He never thought to ask why Amanda was home during the day and I wasn't about to bring it up. My testicles and I were basking in our moment of glory.

We had the usual guy talk. Mariners, Seahawks, and still pretending to be pissed off about the Sonics' traitorous move to Oklahoma City in 2008. Finally, Alex asked how I came to visit the bar and knew the namesake. Another conversation ensued and I briefed him on the journal owner's connection with the place.

"Are you still dicking around with that?"

"It's interesting. It's taken me to some places I'd never have been." I took a gulp of beer. "Given me thoughts outside of 'life as usual'."

"Like this place," he added. "I never thought I'd live to see the day."

I took a few minutes and told him about Bert, and what a character he is. He seemed amused, if not interested, saying, "You can hear those tales in any bar in any city in the country, Chris."

"Yes, but not this story. This is *my* story. I'm following this for *me*. For once I'm doing what *I* want to do." Alex rolled his eyes, but I persisted.

"Every time I've wanted to do something that was a little different or didn't fit into Amanda's rules for life, it was stupid. Or a Walter Mitty fantasy, or a waste of time. Maybe she's right, but this is mine."

Alex said, "If you really want to find this guy, hire the people that run porn sites."

I knew I was in for another of Alex's tales. I started to talk, and at first nothing came out. Finally, I mustered, "I'm afraid to ask, but … what the hell are you talking about?"

Satisfied that I'd bit, he sat up straight, faced me, and began.

"Are you kidding? There's not a site out there that doesn't track users, and porn sites are the best—or worst—depending on your view." He lowered his voice and looked around the bar for dramatic effect.

Alex was in his element. A latter day Mark Twain. If Mr. Twain was a little disturbed.

"Those people know *everything*. You so much as click on a titty pic and it's like being put into a CIA database or something."

I just shook my head. "Why are you on those sites, and how do you know all of this?"

"Really, Chris? I live online. I work online. All my articles are posted online. I get paid by how many people read my shit. Want more proof?" Alex said holding up open palms and staring at me as if I had three eyes.

"I can go to any site where I've created an account and it will ask me to sign in. User name, password, and the like. If I mess up any of those fields, it's back to square one." He took a breath, then in one long, rambling sentence, said, "Please enter your email address or your password hint, blah, blah, blah. Then, click submit and a screen comes up asking me, 'what country do I live in,' and I try it again. I enter USA. It asks for my zip. I enter it. It then asks for my city. I enter it. Then, even after all that, it asks what state."

Seemingly exasperated just going through this, he continued, "Now, if I visit a porn-site? First thing I see is, "Hey, Alex, you middle-age balding guy living right off the I-5 freeway. Call right away, and we'll send someone over. You won't even have to move your truck from space 386. She'll street-park by the grocery store and come in via the mailbox entry hall. P.S., you are low on gas."

He paused, smiling for effect, then added, "You tell me they can't find someone." He stopped long enough to take a swig of beer before heading off on another tangent.

"This reminds me, you remember that smoking little hottie we saw a few years back at that hotel bar during the writers' convention? God, she was bee-u-tee-ful. Remember that skirt? It was so short I could smell the hem."

I wasn't sure what to say, so I went with, "She was awfully young, Alex."

"They let her into the bar, didn't they? Let's face it, she was a party girl, Chris. Don't try spinning this into a case of rocket science. She probably starts out her evenings wearing size six panties, but by midnight they morph into size twenty-two because they fall off at the sound of a beer can popping."

"You're going to go to jail someday, you know that, right?"

He just laughed.

I took a sip of beer. "Pervert."

He didn't respond and just let it drop. This surprised me because when someone doesn't horselaugh over one of his stories, Alex is pretty good about approaching it from different angles until he gets the desired guffaw. He must finally be breaking out of his second puberty.

We chatted for a while longer before I told him I needed to get going. Naturally he jumped on the opportunity to get in a last jab.

"Afraid Mom is waiting for you?" I didn't take the bait. Just thanked him for the beer and slipped on my jacket.

I got the bartender's attention and said, "Beers are on him." I looked at Alex and said, "You have more time than me, remember? I have to get home to Mom."

~

Early the following week, Alex called with a typical Alex proposal. He felt bad about how we'd left things at Bert's and offered to let me buy the beer if he chose the place. How thoughtful.

We met at The Goat, Alex's haunt of choice. I didn't know if the place was named for a person or if the owner just liked goats. Either way, I loved it, goat being one of my favorite words. The Goat was a pseudo-sports bar at the edge of the mall. I say "pseudo-sports" as it's the first one I'd been in that didn't have a TV, but *bar* it certainly was. The only immediate downside I noticed was the music playing from an old Wurlitzer jukebox in a far corner over by the crappers. It reminded me of the problem many singers have: They just don't know when to keep their mouths shut. Off-key, but unfortunately, on-stage. The jukebox was appropriately located.

Alex was there when I arrived, chatting it up with the bartender and no doubt running up my tab. The bartender looked like every bartender you've seen in any noir movie from the 1940s. Indifferent; a background figure with a rag tossed over a sagging shoulder. His eyes darted, on alert for any action. Pretending to know nothing about nothing. Giving a rinse to the three or four empty tap glasses at the end of the bar, he could likely make out any conversation in the room. I ordered a local and wiggled my way to comfort on a barstool. Alex introduced me to Paul, the bartender, I acknowledged him with a tip of my bottle in his direction, and then turned to Alex.

With my best coquettish smile I asked, "Do you come here often?" This, naturally, got me an earful of macho, he-man replies before he added a bit more sarcasm with a raised pinky toast as we clinked bottles.

We made small talk for a while and drained our beers. Alex grabbed the bartender's attention for another round and Paul swung into action. As he dropped bottles in front of us, I took the opportunity to ask him how the place got its name. "Easy. GOAT. The Greatest Of All Time."

Well, didn't I feel foolish.

He turned his attention to Alex. "Have you heard from Hore lately?"

"Not for some time. I figured he'd been poking his head around here or Bert's," Alex said. "I used to run into him around town but haven't seen him since Yeti was spotted romping around the Cascades. He's the hide and seek world champion." We chuckled at the local joke and continued whittling away at the clock.

I was on a mental timer and Amanda would have questions if I didn't arrive home sober, soon, and with an alibi. Sitting there it dawned on me what they had been talking about. I must have done a double-take like an actor in one of those old-time scratchy black and white movies because they stopped talking and stared at me.

"Wait a minute," I said, holding up my hand as if taking an oath. "Hold on a second. You were talking about whore. Whore like a member of the world's second oldest profession or Hore like a nickname?"

Both Alex and Paul seemed confused.

"What the hell are you talking about, Chris?" Alex asked.

"Hore. This Hore guy. Is that his name or a nickname?"

"Alex," I said, thumping his left arm with a backhand. "The journal."

He seemed confused. "The journal I found in the desk. The guy I'm looking for. His name—his nickname or whatever. Hore."

Paul chimed in, "Small world. That old fart has been coming here for years."

"So, wait," I said, a bit confused. "If this is the same guy, then——?" I broke it off at that, hands out, palms up, not sure what to say next.

"It's probably not the same guy, Chris," Alex Said.

"Yeah," I said. "Hore is such a common name, right?" I took a deep breath, slowly exhaling like a puffer fish, before continuing. "I'd just like to know. I've put a lot of time into this fantasy of mine as Amanda calls it, and I'd love some resolution." The two of them stared at me as though I was speaking Klingon.

"So, where can I find this guy? What does he look like? Toss me a bone."

"Not sure what to tell you, son," Paul said. "He comes in, he drinks, he hits the head, and then he leaves. Not like I'd been taking notes or following the guy into the shitter." Both he and Alex chuckled.

"Look, this isn't all that funny to me. And this isn't exactly what I do for a living. I write about sports. I bitch about things people wearing uniforms whine about while they're collecting multi-million dollar paychecks. This—this whole thing is personal for me."

"And," I added, raising my left index finger, "I'm going to see it through."

Neither Alex nor Paul spoke. Only the chatter of other patrons and the faint radio broadcast of a random soccer game filled the air. Apparently I wasn't the only one who didn't enjoy the multi-pitch singer that had been attacking us from the jukebox.

I stared at them, they stared at me, like puppies not sure if they are in trouble or getting a treat. "Well, okay, *maybe* it's not the same guy, but … would one of you let me know if he comes in? I'd like to ask him myself. Don't bring it up to him. Last thing I need is someone else calling me a crackpot."

I left The Goat and did something against my routine and what figured to be a marital faux-pas. I drove along the one way street until I reached Robin Avenue, turned left, then left again on another one way until I hit Bert's on my right. I parked and thought for a moment. Deciding that I could either sit and listen to the rain pelt the roof of my truck or do something, I got out, locked the truck, flipped up the lid of my hoodie, and headed into Alvareza's.

I grabbed a bean and cheese burrito along with a bag of tortilla chips and side of guacamole then headed over to Bert's. I reckoned I'd already lost most of the day's marital points I could lose with Amanda, and, frankly, I wasn't ready for a confrontation. Bert was out for a bit, but was told he was due back any moment. I ordered a diet pop to wash down my late lunch. The bartender looked at me with a touch of disdain. Probably because I'd brought in eight bucks worth of food and ordered a two-buck pop. I figure I got away with it because I'd asked for Bert by name.

As if on cue, Bert strolled in ten minutes later, around 3:40 p.m. I sucked the hot sauce off my fingers, waved, and motioned to talk with him. He gave me the universal, "I see you" nod, and headed towards what I assumed was his office.

By the time I'd polished off my beverage, Bert had swung around the corner and was heading in my direction. I told him about my experience at The Goat and asked if any of it rang a bell. After flipping me crap about going to a semi-competitive bar (because "No place can compare to Bert's!"), we talked about Alex, about Hore, about The Goat, about what the bartender, Paul, had said, and about what I was up to.

Like others, Bert was skeptical of why I was pursuing it, wondered what my motives were, and just couldn't see the relevance or significance to any of it. I told him I respected that, and, to be honest, most everyone else thinks I have an odd fixation as well. At the top of that list: My wife.

He signaled the peace sign to the bartender who momentarily appeared with two bottles of ale. I told him it wasn't necessary but he replied that it wouldn't do well for his business to be seen sitting at his own bar with someone that had a diet cola in front of them. I replied that it wouldn't do well to be giving the goods away—my way of letting him know he just bought them.

Bert said that he had a few things to attend to and maybe we could get together later in the week. I checked my phone and realized I'd been out of the birdcage for nearly five hours and needed to get home. I said I'd give him a call later during the week, or maybe Saturday.

"I've got your number, remember? If I get a chance, I'll give you a buzz," he said. "You can come by my place sometime where I have more time to chat."

We shook hands, I polished off the beer, then headed home, hoping there wasn't already a blanket over my cage. It gets mighty chilly on that couch.

When I arrived, Ama was sitting up in her reading chair. She said she was feeling a little better, but her nose and eyes gave her away. I promised a quiet night in, as I had a bit of catch-up work to do. She didn't argue or question my whereabouts, so I knew from experience that while she claimed to be feeling a little better, she was not yet on her "A" game. She stood, shuffled over to our brown over-stuffed sofa, and curled her way into a tight ball of human cuteness. I headed to my office and ate up an hour working on my column before shutting down my PC. When I returned to the living room, Amanda was asleep on the couch, still in the fetal position. I draped an afghan over her then followed my PC's lead and went to bed.

Celia Browne

I tracked down three local Celia Browne possibilities, eliminating two with just a couple of polite phone calls, before settling on one without an address. I called and she agreed to meet. Didn't ask me any questions, just accepted the call and made an appointment for 9 a.m. in just two days' time. Odd, but maybe I was catching a break. That's the way it always worked for Philip Marlowe.

By her directions, she was about thirty-five miles north, just off of I-5. With my truck in the shop for some new shoes, Alex offered (well ... agreed) to taxi me around. I dropped off the truck at 8 a.m. sharp and walked over to The Goat, which, I was beginning to think, never closed.

I ordered a bottle of sparkling water, which was delivered with the obligatory arched eyebrow and shrug. I killed it and hit the head so I'd be ready to deal with Alex and his, well, let's just say, his outlook on life.

He was slouched over a high-top table when I returned from the crapper.

"I've been waiting," he said, drumming his left index finger on the wooden table to the rhythm of the bar's chugging air conditioner.

"Sitting here for five goddamn minutes."

I picked up the sticky bar menu and flipped it over a few times. "My prostate didn't really set its timer to your arrival."

"Listen, you asked for *my* help. A little respect, please."

I tossed the laminated sheet on the table and looked for a peace offering. "Let's eat," I said, "My treat."

In the entire time I've known Alex he has never been a people person. Describing him as a tall, heavy-set, brooder would paint him in a good light. He was on his third wife and still driving his first car. The Goat was his kind of place, but not today.

"You should have already had breakfast. It's after eight."

The air conditioner groaned, fighting just to wave stale air around the room. After a lengthy pause, he added, "What do you do all frigging morning?"

"Hey, it'd be my treat. I figure it's the least I can do for you dragging me around."

"I do appreciate that, but, if you think I'm eating anything that crawls out of that hole," he said, pointing to the kitchen window at the end of the bar, "you are mistaken. I don't care where the bottles from, but when it comes to food I have higher standards. Not many, I'll give you that, but some.

Besides, you think decent food just grows on friggin' trees?"

I wanted desperately to call him on that, but decided not to push my luck and we headed out to his car.

~

I figured the quickest way of finding out about this Hore character was to ask the people familiar with him—starting with the person who owned the house, and by default, the desk.

The address Ms. Brown provided led us into the parking lot of the Sleep Cheep Six Motel. We looked at each other for a few questioning seconds, not sure what to do next. I broke the stalemate by offering to go into the lobby and see if we had the right place.

The desk clerk was a nondescript man past retirement age. I asked if he knew a Celia Browne. He looked at me for a moment before reciting—without checking a computer—"Room seventeen." I waved 'thanks' and we turned in opposite directions as though pacing off for a dual.

Back outside, I found Alex still sitting in his car reading a magazine. He opened the driver-side window and I leaned on the sill like a traffic cop checking on an attractive motorist. I relayed my conversation with the clerk, adding that I was heading out to find room seventeen. We'd found the place without problem, and were early—around 8:50 a.m.—so there was no rush. The Sleep Cheep Six Motel lived down to its name. Dim lights, a part-gravel, mostly pothole parking area with a soft drink machine hawking off-brand soda and over-priced water next to the entrance; its dying bulb flickering like an aging disco strobe.

"I don't think I could stay here," Alex said.

"Why's that?"

"I don't like sixes."

"What does that have to do with the motel?"

Alex looked skyward, exhaled slowly, and said "Six." Lips barely parting.

"So what do you have against the *number* six?"

As if talking to a small child, he said, "First of all, it's an even number. I don't like even numbers. And it also just happens to be the sign of the devil."

"Alex, 666 is the sign of the devil. Not six."

"Yeah? Well I once ran out of gas because I refused to stop at a Philips 66," Alex said as though that were the obvious and definitive checkmate.

I couldn't think of anything that would elevate the conversation so I just gave the window sill a few quick taps, said, "Give me an hour and pick me up out front," and walked off in search of room seventeen.

~

My goal was simple. I figured that Celia Browne was the listed, legal owner of the house where I bought the desk and where this whole thing started. She could solve this for me and improve my marriage in the process.

I found the room and employed my ritual shave and a haircut on the well-worn door. Smudged around the knob with six to eight inches of grime above the handle, it hadn't been cleaned in a while, or got a lot of use, or both.

A pale, picnic-basket blonde opened without a word.

"Celia?" She nodded and stepped aside for me to enter, curiously, without asking my name.

"I'm Chris," I said, scanning the room. She was an attractive woman with a pretty smile harboring a coquettish edge. She struck me as someone who knows how to get what she wants and has a lot of practice. Back in her high school days, I'd be surprised if she had to buy so much as a single tater tot with her own money.

"You live here?"

"Yeah. You might say I work from home," she said, leaning over a small side table, head tilted, removing an earring. "So what can I do with you?" I didn't immediately reply, watching as she struggled to remove the earring's back post.

She noticed my observation and answered an unasked question. "When I was a child, my dad didn't want me to get my ears pierced," she said, wincing as she pulled the earring from her lobe. "He said girls my age didn't do that. He said *nice* girls my age didn't do that."

She looked me up and down then asked, "So, why are you here? It's not often people make appointments two days in advance. I'm usually more of an urgent thing."

"I bought a desk out in Sublimity a short while back—"

"Congratulations. Did I win the lottery or do you have a point, Mr. … ?"

Her demeanor had flipped like a light switch. "Chris. Just call me Chris. Anyway, it seems the desk had some papers in it and I'd like to find their rightful owner. Marion County tells me that's you."

"Maybe Marion County is in error, Mr. Chris."

"I'm not trying to stir anything up, Ms. Browne. I just want to return this stuff and hopefully find out a little bit more about the owner."

"Call me Celia, and listen, here's the deal. That house, as I'm sure you've figured out, belonged to my so-called father. It was signed over to me and I put it up for sale, complete with whatever was in it. Period. End of story. No story, in fact."

I could see this was a soft underbelly and I treaded lightly. "So, how old were you?" I asked.

"When I started hooking?"

That stopped me in my tracks for a heartbeat. Either I missed some obvious signs or was a little slow on the uptake. "When you got your ears pierced."

"I don't remember," she said, pausing with the earring between her index finger and thumb. "Ten or eleven I guess. Anyway, my Mom got her ears pierced a few months *after* I did, so…"

"How'd your father feel about that?"

"Well, I might have been young, but I was smart enough to put two and two together." She said, flashing a wry smile. "When I saw Mom's earrings, I knew things were going to hell in a handbasket."

Having managed to tug off the backs of the earrings, she placed them in a small plastic dish on the edge of a bedside table before continuing, her voice muffled as she entered the room's small bathroom.

"Dad was pretty pissed off." She paused for a moment, then added, "Which wasn't unusual. Even at his best he was never far from his worst. He called my Mom every name in the book. Jezebel, whore, slut. You name it, he used it."

"What did your Mom do?"

"She didn't take it sitting down if that's what you're asking," she said, returning from the bathroom shaking a couple aspirin from a store brand container.

"She screamed right back, yelling about how she was the only one that had the decency to even pretend to be married. I ran to my room, closed the door, and stayed out of sight." She took a breath, then added, "Funny, but one of the things I remember most about it was going to school the next day and asking Ms. Chestnut, my teacher, what a Jezebel was."

"Were you curious about what a whore and slut were?" I asked, instantly regretting having said it.

Laughing, she said, "No, no. I just remember thinking how weird the word *Jezebel* sounded. Like he was calling her a clown or an acrobat or something. I guess I was hoping that it was all okay and they were just having fun."

After an awkward silence, I asked if she knew where I could find her father. She told me that she hadn't spoken with him in years. "Why would I? What would I have gained? I've heard him use the term *Jezebel*. I really didn't need to hear what he'd came up with since."

I stood and grabbed my jacket. "Well, thank you for your time. I appreciate it."

"Hey, it's your dime."

"I want to be respectful of your time. I'm sure you're busy," again saying something I regretted as soon as it escaped my lips.

"Busy what?" She slammed down the lipstick she was applying. "A busy what? Whore? Slut?" Pause. "A *Jezebel*?"

She didn't let me answer. "Well screw you. If I want a goddamn shrink I'll buy one."

"That's not what I meant. I just wanted to thank you for—"

"You know what? It doesn't matter. You got what you wanted. You guys always do. I thought you wanted to talk. Like I was human." She was crying now. "Why interrogate me? Why come here and bring up my family?" She held her chin high and shakily pointed at me. "I should have never even talked to you. Just … leave."

The bathroom door clicked shut. I zipped my jacket and quietly closed the door behind me, leaving the *no moleste* hanger wagging in place.

I headed down the oft-patched sidewalk back towards the lobby. The drizzle matched the despair of Celia's room. While I felt sad for her, I couldn't shake how defensive she was. Those walls weren't coming down soon. Not for me and not for anyone waving a fifty in front of her.

~

It was only 9:20 a.m. and I didn't figure to see Alex rumble up until ten or so. With a little time to spare, I swung by the lobby to grab a daily paper and, figuring as long as I was there, I'd sneak into the free breakfast buffet, which I quickly discovered held its own challenges. A boxing ring square of a room stuffed with doughy, tucked plaid shirts, shorts, socks and sandal-clad vacationers. We were miles from any remote type of touristy stuff and that in itself should have been enough to warn me away from the food.

There was subtle jostling for the Hope Diamond of stale doughnuts and it seemed everyone in the room was pulling levers to dispense cereal, pushing buttons, twisting knobs, working a wheezing carafe pump, or flipping an electric waffle maker. CNN droned on the wall-mounted TV display. The hot-cup slurping, spoon-and-fork clanking rhythms, juice that wasn't, and obligatory kids on tiptoes stretching index fingers to scoot, flip, or wiggle chocolate-like donuts within grasp (while managing to dredge a mini-fingerprint in them all) marched on.

I wasn't as hungry as I'd thought, and that complimentary breakfast wasn't as appealing as I'd hoped. Something told me it probably wasn't all that free either as I suspect many of the participants would be paying for it later in the day. I couldn't for the life of me imagine what those folks could possibly be on vacation *from*. I still had a few minutes to kill, so I grabbed a Styrofoam to-go cup of coffee, slipped into a corner chair, and watched the carnival while downing the mud.

When I emerged, Alex was waiting out front as promised. I answered his barrage of questions saying simply that Ms. Browne and I had talked and I then spent some time watching people fight over entry-level breakfast items. He looked at me just as I'd looked at him about his number six phobia. Now even, we headed back to the tire shop for my truck.

"So, what did you learn?"

"That she has no interest in the house, the desk, or her dad."

"Her dad. Huh. Interesting. Nothing else? Dead-end?"

"Maybe. Not my job to save the world. You ready to eat?"

Bert's Abode

Bert called on Thursday.

"Why don't you swing by my place this afternoon around four? I'll take a few hours off before the night crowd."

Sensing my hesitation, he added, "I just like to get to know people that come in. You've been by a few times, haven't caused any problems, and thought maybe I'd buy you one … 'on the house,' so to speak."

I accepted.

His place was little hard to find, one of seven or eight small, shingled cottages on a side street just off the beaten path, opposite a trailer park (concrete and faux grass), and nudging a four-lane leading in and out of Salem. His two-bedroom dwelling smelled of smoke, but he never lit up so it might have been residual from his bar, his laundry, or person or persons unseen. There was a sagging sofa and mismatched side chair, end table, a coffee table that had seen better days, and a small TV on a perch by the door. All chairs and tables pointed in the TV's general direction. Wood floors with a couple of tattered area rugs tossed in for ambiance. There was an overhead light fixture, but he seemed to prefer table lamps. We were enjoying a sunny Northwest afternoon, dust mites dancing in shafts of light poking through the blinds on the picture window next to the front door. No ashtray in sight.

We chatted a while as I struggled to determine the pre-sex scene. That's my term for a movie where, as example, a man and a woman seemingly want nothing to do with one another, but then, thanks to film editors or time constraints (or just sloppy continuity), are sitting in a garden somewhere professing their undying love and slobbering all over each other. I always call out, "Did I miss the pre-sex scene?" (Much to Amanda's chagrin.)

I was trying to make the connection between being a new customer at his business and being asked over. I'd like to think that I'm chock-full of charisma, but this was hard to fathom.

We jawed for a bit, making small talk. I finally asked him to what did I owe his invitation? He said he'd noticed I'd been coming in to the bar and repeated his earlier comment about wanting to get to know his customers.

"Most people meet in a bar to get to know someone better," he said. "Since that's where I meet *everyone*, I like to take it outside the bar. Can I offer you a beer?" I gave a silent chuckle. "Habit," he said with a smile. "But remember, it's on the house here."

I joked now that I knew where he lived, I'd bypass his bar and just head straight over.

The beer helped with the awkwardness and we kept it high-level. How long had he owned the bar ("eighteen years"), where did I work ("You're Chris is Crossed? Son-of-a-bitch! I read your shit!"), and so on for about thirty minutes.

I drained my beer, checked the time and told him I needed to be heading out.

"Listen, before you go, there's someone I think you should meet."

I looked around the room, my surprise showing loud and clear.

"No, no. Not here. At the bar. Swing by Saturday. There's a character that comes in. Name's Roully. Friends with the guy you're looking for. If nothing, he's a real hoot to talk with."

I told him I'd try to make it in. Didn't know if I had other plans (read: I should check in with the home front), but no way was I going to miss this opportunity. Standing to leave, Bert encouraged me to take a bottle of his homemade wine. He said that everyone liked it, and that the highest praise of all came from a neighbor of his to whom he'd given a few bottles last fall.

Pointing out the window towards another little cottage he said, "Matt, that's his name, told me he'd kept them in his backyard shed over the winter, along with a few home-canned veggies and jams." I had a hunch where this was heading.

"So anyway, Matt said come April, most of his veggies had exploded, but not my wine." Grinning, he turned back from the window. "Nope. My wine was good as new. Fresh, cold, and ready to pour." He looked like the school kid who was taking the hottest girl in class to the dance.

"I'd like to think it was the harsh winter that blew-up his pickles and onions but I know better. I make *real* wine," he said with a wink.

I took him up on his offer, thinking if I could get a glass in Amada's hands that we'd enjoy an uneventful evening. A handshake and wave later, I was in my truck heading home with a bottle of, if Bert wasn't pulling my leg, fortified wine, but my thinking was leaning more towards what could best be described as wineshine. This stuff apparently could be safely stored in a freezer, and, in emergency, used in my truck radiator.

Roully

On Saturday, I slipped out and headed to Bert's Tavern. Stepping in, it took a few seconds for my eyes to adjust to the dim lighting and my nose to adjust to I'm not certain what. Bert was wiping down the far end of the bar and waved me over. We exchanged pleasantries and gabbed for a few minutes.

"Well, just to make me out a liar, I haven't seen Roully today. If you have a bit of time or want to swing by later today—"

I waved my hand. "That's probably a good idea. I have a few errands I should run to keep me out of the dog house. How about I check back in an hour or so, give or take?"

"I'll be here. Can I grab anything for you before you go?"

"Naa. Save one for me though," I said with a smile.

"I may have to," he said. "You don't know what you might be getting into."

My antennae went up. "What do you mean?"

"Well," he said, "Let's just say that you might do well to learn some history about 'ol Roully." He must have sensed my curiosity because he added, "Nothing terribly bad, mind you, just a few things you ought to be aware of." Lowering his voice, he added, "He's not a murderer or anything like that … least I know of, anyway."

I figure he added the wink just to screw with me.

"Anyhoo, go do your errands and I'll give you the lowdown when you get back."

I furrowed my brows a bit, giving my best sixth-grader staring at a hard math problem expression, thanked him, and walked out to my truck.

I really didn't have any specific errands, but knew if I bailed out on a Saturday for more than a couple hours, that it was in my best interest to do so with a purpose other than meeting a stranger—even a male stranger—in a bar. I took the opportunity to swing by the home warehouse and pick up a couple of wood slats needed for the backyard fence. For good measure, I hit the market and grabbed a fresh loaf of jalapeno bread and some dessert treats. By the truck's clock it had been about an hour and fifteen minutes, so I swung back to Bert's, anxious to hear his tale.

When I arrived, Bert was serving a couple of people at a high-top table just off the side of the entrance. He nodded and pointed to the empty space at the end of the bar, where we had chatted earlier. The times I've been there I've noticed that the place was never crowded but never empty. It felt like a neighborhood place should feel.

After a few minutes Bert swung by, beer in hand.

"I didn't order this."

"Relax," he said. "This one is on me. You'll appreciate it by the time Roully finishes with you."

"Ah. So, he has arrived?" I asked, scanning the room.

"Yup. That's him over at the corner table," he said, nodding in the direction of an old, bearded guy sitting alone, working on a beer. "I told him that someone wanted to chat with him about Hore."

"Ah, shit. Did it spook him?"

"Are you kidding me?" Leaning in, "He sees you as an opportunity. You'll learn fast that Roully is out for one person. Roully. If he can milk you for a drink, he'll milk you for the logo on the glass it's served in."

"So, what do you suggest?"

"Look, if you want information, then you'll play his game. It's your call, Chris." He shrugged, then added, "I don't know what you are up to or what you hope to achieve, but if you want an introduction, I'll give it to you. I typically stay out of these things. People come in *here*, he said tapping his index finger on the bar, "to not be out *there*," jutting his thumb towards the entrance.

I told him I surely did want to talk with this guy. I asked if there was anything else I should know or be aware of. Way over the top, I'm sure. I felt like a teenager asking a friend about their sister.

"I'll take you over. But first, let me tell you a little story. Gimme a second."

He walked to the other end of the bar and served up a couple of refills before returning.

"Here's a starter tale for you, Chris," he said, again leaning in. "I've known Roully for some years now. He is the cheapest son-of-a-bitch you will ever meet."

"I don't know, Bert. I've met plenty of cheapskates in my time. Sports writers aren't exactly known for being loose with the greenbacks."

"Well, here you go. He once offered me a very-nice Cuban cigar. Now I like cigars. I *know* cigars. And I was surely surprised. I rarely saw him with a bankroll, and the stick he gave me doesn't come cheap, or legal around these parts. I asked him about it right then, because I didn't want to partake in something he'd obtained under the counter. Running a tavern, that would be a quick way for me to lose my license."

Bert looked over my shoulder towards Roully before continuing. "Well, Roully saw my surprise and looked me right in the eyeballs and said, 'Die big. The fifty centers will kill you, too.' This as he pounded down a shot of single malt. Mind you, all this was *after* I'd loaned him twenty bucks for 'gas' money. He's the stingiest S.O.B I've ever come across, unless it isn't his money on the table. Then you'd have thought he'd invented air."

I must have given quite a look because Bert said, "I told you there were things you should know." He smiled, and added, "You've been warned."

"I appreciate that," I said, standing up and rubbing my hands together like an umpire massaging a new baseball. "I'm anxious to meet this guy. Lead on."

~

"Hey, Roully. This is Chris, the guy I was telling you about."

The man stood, "Pleased to meet you, Chris."

We exchanged pleasantries and introductions, and Bert headed back to the bar. I stood anxiously, until Roully gestured towards a chair. "Sit down for God sake," he said.

The first thing I noticed was his lengthy gray beard. Hard to miss. Sitting, it ran to his nipples. When he stood, the whiskers still rappelled to his collarbone. To generate some non-committal conversation, I asked him about the beard. He said, "Ever since the top of my head started showing, I figured I'd grow it where I got it."

I told him that the few people I'd met with a beard that long are prone to play with it. Stroke it and twizzle it, like women do with their hair. He looked at me like I had spinach in my teeth and said, "I don't need to play with it. I know where it is."

I was trying to figure out if I'd already offended him when he continued. "It's no different than women. You thinks because I got hair that I have to play with it. Like women's titties or something." He nodded at me and continued. "That's something you need to give some thinking to. You can't just stare at a woman's titties. You gotta appreciate them." I couldn't tell if I was getting a canned spiel or if he really was just coming up with this stuff for my benefit. Either way … weird.

"When I see a good-looking woman, I don't just stare at her titties. I focus. I imagine them tiddlywinks and their little tongue bumps. Them silky, fuzzy hairs. You can't really see a woman's titties without wondering if those little hairs mat down like a spider on a shower floor." He paused, pointed at me, and added, "Appreciate. Don't stare."

I wasn't sure what to say, what to make of all this, or what it had to do with anything, but Roully just kept right on talking. "See—women are delicate. Like flowers. You can't just go picking them up and treating them like laurel bushes. You gotta understand that they got nuances and sensitivities. You can't judge a woman by her titties. You see what I'm saying? They ain't just titties. You got to see the whole picture, 'less you're a pervert or something."

I'd known the guy all of five minutes and he was already off the rails and walking on his own path. I listened, not really sure what to say. The best I could come up with was, "Well, I can't really argue with your logic. Women's breasts certainly deserve a place of esteem."

He seemed pleased.

"Bert told you what I was looking to talk about?"

"Yup. Said you're fixin' to do a story on Hore."

"What? No, I'm looking to learn about him and I have something that might belong to him."

"Well, he says you're a-writing something," he said, looking at me with one eye slightly closed.

"No, no, I'm not looking to write about anyone here. I *am* a writer though. A sports writer."

"Well, you're barking up the wrong tree, fella. Old Hore, he can't toss a ball further than the bar over there."

"I bought an old desk at a yard sale out in Sublimity. It had some sports magazines in it along with a journal that I believe belongs to him. I'm just looking to return it."

Roully stared at me, eventually winning the battle of silence.

"Some of the stuff in the notebook, or journal, or whatever it is, is interesting, so yeah, sure. I'm a writer so I suppose that makes me curious as well."

"So what is it you want to know?"

I explained the journal and desk in detail, and told him I was just looking to fill in the blanks and eventually get it back to the owner, whom I assumed was his friend, Hore.

"Tell you what. I'm kind of busy this afternoon, what with life and all. I have time for a quick drink if you'd like, then maybe we can talk a little longer another time." He motioned to Bert.

"Bert, this gentleman has offered to buy a round," he said motioning to me. "What'll you have, son?"

I asked Bert for another of whatever beer I had earlier and to give Roully whatever he'd like.

Roully smiled, "I'll have a finger of Glenlivet." Then after a quick pause added, "You know, go ahead and make it two man-size fingers."

As Bert turned to the bar he gave me the universal *I told you so* expression of raised brows and eyes peering at me as though he were wearing reading glasses. I don't know how much he tried to hide his smile, but it didn't work.

Roully worked on his scotch while I played with my beer. I told him I needed to get going soon, but looked forward to talking with him again. "Just a quickie before I go, though. How is it you know this Hore guy?" I asked still feeling weird about calling a stranger 'Hore.'

"Well, that was many years ago now, son," he said. "Let me tell you a little story about our friendship. One night, a bunch of us were at a bar. Hore, who I'd never laid peepers on before, was obviously too far gone to drive himself home. A few of us followed him out of the bar telling him he ought not to drive. Well, he argued the point all the way to his car, wiggled in, slammed the door, and rolled down the window." Roully paused, smiled slightly, and gave a little sigh before continuing.

"So, Hore sez, 'No problem,' and makes a stab for the Virgin Mary medallion dangling from his rearview mirror. He squinted and tilted his head like one of them confused puppies until he was able to get hold of it, then talked to the damn thing! 'Mary, sweetie, I'm too drunk, you're driving home tonight.' Well, I'd already picked up his keys back in the bar so I just turned around and walked back in to my drink. Don't know where he went or how he got home but he found me a few days later sitting in the same place. Walked up to me and held out his hand. I reached into my pocket, fished out the keys and dropped them in his palm. Feller turned and left. Just like that," he said, snapping his fingers.

He smiled and said I could find him at Bert's most weekends and he would make all the time I needed. I tossed cash on the table, thought better of it, scooped it up, and told him that I'd take care of it at the bar. He smiled and I headed towards home.

~

On the drive, my mind wandered back to a time last summer. I was lazing in a deck chair on the balcony of the hotel room at an ocean front property in Lincoln City, on the Oregon Coast. Ama and I were cherishing a weekend of nothing but sand, ocean roars, and books. If you are familiar with the Northwest coast, you know that walking on the beach is fun. Getting in the water without a wetsuit is not. And with every year you age, that water seems to get about two degrees colder. Generally speaking, most Northwesterners go to the *coast*, not to the *beach*.

Anyway, someone had tossed out a small piece of a roll; baguette maybe. It lay in the sand for the better part of an hour, gently rocking to the will of the ocean breeze. Beachcombers passed, waves punched and jabbed the chilly Northwest shore. Like a miniature statue, the bread remained.

Eventually a seagull waddled over and swallowed it whole, with one muscular gulp. No noise, squawking, flapping, or fluttering wings. Just a quick landing on an otherwise empty beach save a few large pieces of water-soaked driftwood. Then, as though someone flipped a switch, they arrived. Three or four at first, and then twenty or more rapidly appeared, swooping and hovering in search of brunch; reminding me of Hitchcock's classic, *The Birds*, without the evil intent (unless you are a baguette).

People might call them sea rats, but that doesn't make them stupid. They're not as smart as crows, mind you, but street smart in a thuggish way, though they'd be the first to fly to escape a potential confrontation. Opportunistic pickpockets of the sea. Give them a fifteen dollar cigar and a couple fingers of twenty-year-old scotch and I'd probably be throwing 'gas money' at them as well. Yes, Roully was on my mind.

Weeds

Sundays were designated yard and garden days. Designated by Amanda and adhered to by those who wished to glimpse snippets of baseball or football on the tube (post-gardening, naturally) with a modicum of enjoyment. For me, gardening does not come easy. The bending, plucking, and cussing. The weeds. Weeds everywhere. Amanda doesn't seem the least bit annoyed. Even thistles cower before her yard-ninja prowess. Often, it seems she just wills the weeds to surrender.

I mosey along, doing what comes natural, beginning with rummaging through the paint-peeled old wood shed and staying out of sight. The same shed whose door once experienced a near fatal episode on a blustery, rainy afternoon leaving it hanging to life by a bent, rusty hinge, face down— ready for burial. Playing he-man handyman, I repaired the door, reinforcing it with a fistful of wood screws, thus earning a weekend off for good behavior.

On this day I find what I need. A large, manual hedge trimmer and a sturdy nine inch handsaw. Amanda can continue her game of Whack-A-Weed. I hunt limbs and branches. Manly stuff. It's a temporary fix, but I can pull up my jeans and scratch myself as well as any husband in the neighborhood. My goal, as always, was to make a dent. Something that screams, "Check this shit out, baby!" Then be seen picking up the mess as to demonstrate progress. This usually works. I think she just wants me to do what she wants me to do and the results are often superfluous.

We repeat this ritual weekly during spring, summer, and fall months. As much as I loathe snow (and thankful that we usually get little of it), at least I don't have to fight weeds during winter. I do cherish my herb, onion, and tomato harvests, and enjoy picking raspberries from along the fence line. By November though, I've usually had enough. The winter months are time for healing. My back needs rest. The garden will go dormant and we'll play it all out again next spring—the garden as victor, weeds the obligatory villains. My knees defeated, slowly giving way to the recliner, falling back with a resounding thump, toes at eye level; once again acting as gun sights aimed at the large flat-screen TV across the room. To my right, the rusting garden is in view through the unlined curtains off the slider. Ama hopefully sated until April. Life is good.

So, I did my thing, going through the usual motions. The days the lawn needed mowing helped my cause. Progress was visible and immediate. After the lawn, I could usually get away with some *me* time.

Today though, my mind was less on yard work than it was on this Roully character. I wondered: How much does he want to talk about his assumed buddy, Hore; how much he wants to talk in general; and how much money he thinks he might squeeze from me. He knows I am a sports writer so I assume that he also knows there isn't a lot of juice to be squeezed. I do believe he has some information about my mystery man or Bert wouldn't have introduced us. That he knows how to milk another man's bar tab, was also not in question. Interestingly though, I was deciding that I really didn't mind so much.

Time Stops For No One

That evening, Amanda had homework so I trundled back to my office. My Dad had called earlier while I was working out in the yard. I missed his call, but got the voicemail. Though it was a normal, 'Hey, how are you doing' call, his voice seemed old. Sounded old.

Dad is older than Mom by nine years, and she had me at thirty-four. Running the numbers I realized that time was running short. In my head, he'll always look the same. Same guy playing catch with me. Same guy chewing me out when I was a teenager and still knew everything. But the voicemail was a wake-up call. He was old.

The silence between our generations blanketed any real connection. We spoke mostly through jokes and things we saw on TV that we could point at and laugh about together. He taught me the basics, no question. I close my eyes and there he is—Dad, all those years ago. The Dad that cussed me out when I was late, and taught me manners: "Yes, sir, no sir, yes ma'am, please, and thank you."

Whenever someone I know passes away—an old classmate, co-worker, or a cousin perhaps—I mentally run through the numbers comparing my age to theirs. If you don't do it now, believe me, as you get older, you will. Time catches up with all of us. I'm still in my working years with retirement on the far horizon. I feel great and convince myself that I can still do everything I could during my high school years. I'd probably be much better on subject-matter tests, but would undoubtedly fail gym class. When I run now, I don't go any faster, I just make more noise. If I were to jump? You wouldn't be able to slide a piece of paper under my feet. A complete reversal of how it was back then.

Why teens don't perceive me as a peer becomes all-too-obvious whenever I encounter a mirror. I have to face the notion of aging and of not having done much of what I just *knew* I was going to do as an adult.

I'm not a Wall Street baron nor a rock star. The only undies at my feet are my own. I reluctantly confess to looking into my bathroom cabinet and realizing I'd never have to buy another comb in this lifetime. Bald? No. I just know the plastic comb will outlast me. I wonder if others feel this way, but it isn't really a good conversation starter. "Hi. I'm Chris. Do you ever think about mortality, aging, and being dead?" Besides being creepy, it sounds like the lead to a burial policy sales pitch. Perhaps Hore feels this way. That his journal, such as it is, is important to him—as much of a diary as it is about the people he owes money to or those owing him money—was obvious. His notes are random, yet orderly. Concise, but telling a story.

I can relate.

Looking around my office I realized it wasn't just my comb. I'd never need another chair or another desk or mini-blinds or area rug. They will all outlast me. I could only win the endurance battle by purchasing newer items of similar ilk and giving these new homes. Then again, that's just reshuffling the same deck of cards. I only hope that I will continue to need additional photo frames and maintain the mental faculty to recognize the significance of their contents. My father's voicemail still stuck in my craw, I decided right then that I needed to take a break and make a trip home.

Missouri

Amanda was studying for finals and I was obsessed with the Hore journal thing. I thought a little space might do both her and me some mental good. This was a great opportunity to pay my parents a short visit. Having retired to a small, rural town in mid-south Missouri, my only challenge was getting from Lambert-St. Louis International to their home, some 170 miles from the terminal and three and a half hours of driving, mostly on two-lane roads.

Why Missouri? Well, no one can tell their family where to live, and every-so-often that means plane rides to Missouri. And, in my best Seinfeld voice, I add, "Not that there's anything wrong with that." When trying to explain where my folks live—that it's a small, rural town with limited cell service, no malls, and few things to do besides watch antennae TV—people assume they live in the backwoods, surrounded by people crapping squirrel meat and pissing moonshine. I get their point, but it's actually a pretty laid back, "how do you do," small town with a welcoming atmosphere.

I made a rare trip up to the newspaper office to make a cameo and do a courtesy round. Shake hands, how are you, how's the family, good to see you, stuff like that. Working from home, I'm already a bit of a ghost. When I disappear for a few weeks at a time though, my Spidey senses always remind me to show up in person to let everyone know I'm still alive and kicking.

As I was heading out, someone said to make sure and say howdy to their cousin in Kansas City. Really?

As long as there are globes, someone will think you have someone in common if you are within five-hundred miles of them. If I travel to London, surely I've heard of their family in Cornwall. Oregon? Obviously then, I'm intimate friends with their kooky brother in Portland. They hear someone mention a place that resonates ... Oregon or England or Missouri or the moon, and immediately believe I *must* know the same people, same buildings, same ... everything.

"You saw the light at Elm Street turn red to green? Me too!" One minute they want to beat the holy crap out of a person and the next they learn they've been to the same state park, and suddenly— presto-chango—they're best friends.

Thus began my trip to the "hill people." A term I learned from the narrator of a TV show where people were sticking fireworks in bodily orifices where fireworks don't belong, and pissing on lit gas cans. It is a bit more colorful than *redneck* and less disrespectful than *hillbilly*, so "hill people" has stuck in my craw—so to speak.

~

Portland International Airport (or PDX) was no busier than usual and the security line and TSA agents were busy *as* usual. Since the tragedy of 9/11, it's difficult to get on a plane (and *out* of an airport, if you're traveling to a place requiring a passport). The days of meeting loved ones at their gate have become nostalgic memories of yesteryear. I figure these are small prices to pay for helping assure passenger and aircraft safety.

The planes themselves are another matter. Shrinking seats and legroom, charging for baggage, meals, farting, headphones, and anything else the powers-that-be figure we humans might enjoy. I wonder how much longer before those teeny-weeny things they call lavatories have quarter slots on the doors, like bus stations of old. (Don't worry, if you don't have a quarter, the flight attendants will make change—for a 10% service fee.)

I had an aisle seat, the person next to me didn't try to chat me up, the person in front of me didn't put their seatback in my face, the person across the aisle didn't take off her socks and shoes, no baby cried, no one brought smelly food aboard, and no one used my seatback as a springboard to walk up and down the aisle. All in all, a decent flight. An on-time arrival with a decent landing was the cherry topping.

I wound my way through the corridors of Lambert (STL for those keeping score at home) making my way to the rental car area. As a side note, I'd always found it odd that Charles Lindbergh Field is in San Diego while St Louis' airport is named for Albert Lambert, an Olympic golfer. In all fairness though, Lambert took flying lessons from Orville Wright (yes, that one), and Lambert Field, as it's commonly known, was the first municipal airport in the United States—so, some major props and serious runway cred there (insert rim shot). If you're still reading, and care, San Diego gave its airport the Lindberg moniker as a tip of the cap to Lindbergh's plane, the Spirit of St. Louis, as it was built in San Diego by Ryan Airlines. Moving along ...

After jumping through the obligatory airport and rental car hoops, I was on my way to Mom and Dad's place. An old-fashion, slow-clock berg of five-hundred three souls (plus goats and cows). Quiet. Frog-belching quiet, and not so much as a Walmart within fifty miles.

It was uncomfortably warm, as many summer days are in the middle-west; astronomical humidity compounding things. With the majority of neighborhood windows open, you could hear the familiar sound of toilet seats slamming as they succumb to gravity, liberating themselves from the sticky behinds of throne bearers from Sycamore

Avenue to East Main Street. My folks call those clammy bathroom adventures, "seat poppers." That was shorthand gist of the day's weather forecast.

After last winter's unseasonable (and, I add, *unreasonable*) snow, I told myself, and everyone within earshot, that I would never again bitch about the heat. An obvious lie, but, as it doesn't often hit ninety-octane on the thermometer in Keizer, I believed it a safe roll of the dice. Now, in fairness, aside from a few jumps off the wagon, I have kept my vow. And to this day, I much prefer ninety degrees Fahrenheit to ten. Or twenty. Or thirty. Or even forty. And snow. Well, snow is the X-factor. As a kid, snow served the useful purpose of closing schools. As an adult—it shuts down any activity a decent, suntanned person over the age of thirty-five enjoys. I don't do snow forts, snowballs, snow angels, snowmen, snowmobiles, or snowshoes. I don't like to walk in it, drive in it, ski on it, or sled on it. Other than that, snow is just ducky.

And then, I got off the plane in St. Louis.

Today, snow was not on my mind. Today required gloves, not the kind for snowball fights. The kind used to avoid blisters when you touch the steering wheel. A day so hot you couldn't wear shorts because you'd fry the back of your thighs climbing into your car. But I hadn't worn shorts on the plane, so I was sweaty hot, not scalding hot in the rental.

The weather, especially when you are not accustomed to it, chains you with oppression. An unjust smothering, sticky weight between teasing, gasping breezes. Sweltering, entrenched among the horizon-leaning rows of Midwest farm corn. Today, I am dripping and tugging at my tee, yearning for stiff wind and a baby-bathwater warm rain. It is hot, hot, hot. The kind of hot that when night falls, brown recluse spiders just weakly nod and tell you to poison yourself.

And then there are bugs. Gnats? Fleas? Corn chiggers? I'm not up on my entomology. I do know they stick to sweat like gravel dust to a damp windshield. Mosquitoes—and they raise 'em big here—are my real nemesis. We maintain a rocky, turbulent, yet intimate relationship. If they aren't trying to kill me, I am trying to kill them.

I have since learned to identify wasps, hornets, and other nasty flying kamikaze critters. If mosquitoes are infantry, hornets and wasps are where the insect military really invests. Those little bastards are unmistakable and maintain a take-no-prisoners approach to farm and field warfare. Kill or be killed. I often wonder if the survivors sit around in little wasp bars, chugging wasp beers, and talking about that time they nearly got knocked out of the sky by a broom.

~

Mom was fine. (As I read through this I realize I speak mostly of my Dad. No disrespect to Mom, God love her. This was just one of those occasions that I needed to have some time with Dad.) At my age I find myself looking for answers to questions that I didn't even know existed in my teen years. I left home knowing everything, and now realize the older I get, the smarter my parents get.

Mom is the foundation. The building block and the more practical of the parental units. She also has a way of giving life lessons without me even knowing what she was up to until years later. As example: When I was a young teen, as we'd sit down for dinner (or supper as it was called), she'd often say, "Remember, if you only taste with your mouth, you are missing most of life." Then she'd look around the table, eventually making eye contact with me and point with her fork, adding, "Chew wisely." To this day that pops into my head whenever I'm perusing a restaurant menu. It always brings a smile and never fails to engage my mind.

Dad? Well, he's the outlier, and that's what I needed. A bit of time to kick through the leaves, so to speak. As always, he was a handful. He'd spent nearly a week in a hospital fighting pneumonia and was now anxiously, restfully, back in his own home. He could smoke and fart and cuss out the president, laugh at racist jokes, and complain about everything he didn't agree with and some that he did.

When I was growing up, there was a time I didn't understand him, the times I didn't agree with him, and now it just doesn't all matter much at all. If Dad told me a racist joke, I wouldn't cringe. I'd just look to the source, and—good or bad—that's my father. Today, those type of jokes are not politically correct.

But my dad spent his formative years smack dab in the mid-1940s and for better or worse, things were much different in those days. That leaves the choice of alienation or acceptance. I chose the latter. When Dad told any type of joke, it was simply because it was a joke. He didn't know any different and never had. Doesn't make him a saint, but it doesn't make him evil either. There was a time I didn't know any different either. I do now, but he never will. And I've come to terms with that. We can't choose our parents and, by the time we arrive on the scene all fresh and gooey, it's a little late to be trying to change them. Sure, we can *train* them, heck, they might not even notice. A diaper here, a car seat there, next thing you know, we run the place (until that inevitable epiphany when we realize that, as eighteen-year-olds, we know everything about everything).

~

"Hey, Chris, what's the difference between car tires and a black guy?" he'd ask. "Tires don't start singing gospel songs when you put chains on them."

I'd heard it so many times that it became accepted. Not acceptable; *accepted.* Then again, this isn't a discussion about political correctness or sensitivity. It's my story and that's the way it was. To avoid it or pretend it wasn't so, would be just as big of a lie as pretending slavery hadn't existed. That joke has been in my head for years, and yes, there were times I've wanted to repeat it. Not because it was racist, but simply because I learned it from Dad. What did I know? He was (is) my dad and I was a kid (there's a lesson in there for today's parents). Then, suddenly it seemed, the world grew up. Jokes became wrong. Words became letters and hyphens. The N-word. Funny became mean. If you held an opinion, you learned to keep it to yourself. To paraphrase Mark Twain, "Only the dead can afford to speak their minds."

It's strange how all that works. Seems one way to make a fortune is to tell the world all the things that have become taboo or publicly flammable, whether it's something you personally believe or not. You'll be labeled a shock jock and through it, your growing audience—your lovers and your haters—will make you richer and richer and you'll preach louder and harder. Some of these soap box pundits tell stories of how you can get more sex than ever, some assert how the republicans are evil and some tell how democrats want to give it all away or how minorities are asking too much from the government or how white rights are being brushed aside.

Like clothing fashions or car styles, these shock jocks and preachers and pundits slowly fall out of style (some re-emerging for a new audience down the line). They leave behind a gaggle of listeners more desperate, longing, and neglected than ever. They were alone and desolate and searching. All having believed in *the voice*. And the voice deceived them. Those voices, now entrenched in their pricey homes paid for by the very people they lured. I know, I know … I've lost my train of thought again, haven't I?

~

So, Mom is fine. Dad is Dad. Hasn't learned a new joke or found a politician he likes in seventy-some odd years. I grabbed a couple of lite beers from the fridge, handed one to Dad and we plopped down on the living room sofa for a bit. While there's a romantic, nostalgic feel to sitting outside on a porch during a Midwestern evening, the reality is, there are mosquitoes and other bug-like things on the other side of the screen. Waiting. Carrying my photo around under their wings.

After popping the tops we enjoyed a few minutes of quiet. I'd never been especially close to my dad. I love baseball. He loathes sports. (As years go by, I've learned to appreciate that him playing catch with me as a kid was a true demonstration of love.) I, naturally, liked "popular" music while he preferred bluegrass or old school country. He never missed an opportunity to remind me that all the songs I listened to sounded alike. And, as I get older, much of *today's* music sounds alike to me. Every so often, I'll check out videos online just to get a feel for what's hot. Some of these videos (I'm old enough to remember when MTV aired music videos), have more than ten million views and they don't sound any different than any other song. So—touché. Here's to you, Dad.

We talked cussing for a bit. Interesting topic, I know. Specifically, I asked him about a childhood incident.

"Dad, you know—you swear a lot. Not that I'm judging, mind you. Lord knows that's where I got it from."

He looked at me and said, part serious, part sardonically, "Well, by God, you did *not* get it from me. Your Mom would have chopped my nuts off if I swore around you. You might have a nasty mouth, but, no siree, you didn't learn that shit from me."

I drained my beer, stood, and headed for the kitchen. Pausing at the doorway, I turned back, leaned on the doorjamb and asked, "You remember me coming home from grade school—probably seven years old. That day Mrs. Jenkins called you?"

He looked at me, and I could see he was searching his memory, so I helped him out. "She was my teacher, and she called because I said 'fuck' in class. Well, you were royally pissed. I remember like it was yesterday. You know why I remember? Because you asked me where I'd learned such a word and I told you I heard it working in the garage with you."

He didn't say anything, waiting for me to fill in the blanks. "It wasn't until I was older and thought more about it, that the answer I should have given was, 'Well, you send me to school all week and Mom sends me to church on Sunday. The teacher was the one who ratted me out, so you do the math." He chuckled, his chest and small belly moving up and down.

"Yeah, I remember. I guess I might have had something to do with it, but I sure couldn't 'fess up to your Mother though. She is one ornery woman when she puts her mind to it."

~

It was getting dark and most of the flying and crawling critters had abated, so we ventured outdoors and settled on the front porch.

Looking around, I said, "I'd forgotten just how big this yard is."

"Nearly an acre."

"And you're still mowing it?" I asked.

"Why not?" he shrugged. "The mower works just fine."

"That push-mower you've had for, like, twenty years? Are you nuts?"

I had no idea that my father was still doing this. I was ashamed that I didn't know and embarrassed that I hadn't made other arrangements.

"Have you thought about a riding mower? I'd be happy to buy one for you."

"Nah, she works fine. And it's paid for," he added before taking a sip of beer. "These days, it just takes me a little longer to get it cut."

I thought about it for a second, envisioning my aged father pushing a mower around an acre of yard. "I'm offering to buy a riding mower. It too would be paid for, Dad."

"I don't need my kid buying me a frigging lawn mower. What I have works."

I tried a new tact.

"Have you and Mom considered selling this place and moving into a decent retirement home?"

He looked at me as though I were a six-eyed alien from planet Zork.

"Son, I appreciate your concern, I really do. If it makes you feel any better, your Mom did check into one a short while back. Said they had a waiting list. I told her to tell them we all are on life's waiting list. They wanted a deposit plus first and last month's rent." He forced a short, chest-jerking laugh. "Shit, at my age, the first and last month could be the same thing. How do you calculate that?

"Chris, understand, we've been here so many years now. We own this place." He gazed around the yard, across the road, and towards the sky before adding, "This is home. I can pay someone to mow the lawn. Hell, I could fly you out here to mow the damn thing for what those retirement homes want to gouge me for a couple small rooms." He relaxed a bit in his chair.

"Retirement home." He squeezed his eyebrows together and looked skyward. "Chris, I am retired and I am home." Then, waving away a kamikaze mosquito, added, "Besides, I still have all my own teeth."

I chuckled a bit at that, but kept it as quiet as I could. Looking up at Dad, I saw he was laughing as well.

That was the last of that.

The topic eventually came around to my job and how I was doing. I told him it was good and that I was certain that this was the Cubbies' year. It was a running joke for as long as I can remember. Actually, a twofold joke. First, because the Cubs haven't had "their year" since 1908, and second, Dad could no more tell you who Ernie Banks was than he could who invented the two-piece bathing suit. Truth be told, I bleed Cubbie Blue and they have a decent team these days. If they ever manage to win it all, I'll cry like a baby.

I shared the story of the journal, and my quest to find its owner. Unexpectedly, instead of telling me I was foolish, he was interested and asked a lot of questions. *What am I doing? Where am I looking? What does Amanda think? Why am I looking? What do I hope to achieve?*

Eventually, he said, "Let me ask you this, Chris," pondering for a moment as if trying to find the easy way into this. "What will you do if you find this guy? What would you say to him? 'Hey, I found some of your personal shit, went through it, and have been stalking you ever since.' Would that work?"

He took a sip of beer, tilted his can in my direction, and continued. "I'm not suggesting that what you're doing isn't worthwhile. Maybe it gets you out of the house, gives you something to do, feeds your inner Sherlock or whatever. I *am* suggesting that you think about what you'll do or say when or if you ever meet this guy." He sat back and we were both quiet for a minute or two. Then, he shared a cautionary tale with me.

"You remember your Great-Aunt Janice?"

I replied that I did. She was a grand lady who fell victim to Alzheimer's. Sweetest person you'd ever want to meet.

"Beautiful lady, dad. Very spiritual person."

He looked at me for a second, then said, "Well, there's a lesson for you."

"You lost me, Dad. What do you mean?"

"A few years before she passed," he said, "and long after she'd been diagnosed, she was home alone for a short spell and had an incident. Seems the kitchen sink sprouted a leak. Well, Janice flipped through the yellow pages, found a plumber, and called for an emergency appointment."

I thought about this for a moment and not seeing any relevance, shrugged and said, "So …?"

"Well," he said pausing for a taste of beer. "That plumber showed up. Janice let him in, showed him the leak, and left him to his business. She apparently went into her bedroom to tackle some chores. When she went back into the kitchen, she found a man under her sink, screamed and began swinging at him with a skillet."

I said that I didn't understand and dad replied that that was the point. "Neither did your great-aunt. Her disease had progressed to the point that she didn't remember calling a plumber, inviting him in, or having him in the kitchen. While, in its own way, that has a touch of humor in it, don't miss the big picture."

"That she was ill?"

"There's more to it than that," Dad said, sitting forward in his chair. "And as the plumber learned, innocently enough, you never know what you're getting into. See, you've been doing a hell of a lot of snooping and he might not be all that pleased about it. He might just beat the shit out of you or pull a gun," he said, loosening his grip on the beer enough to jab his index finger in my direction.

Dad made some good points and gave me a lot to think about. I certainly have no ill-will toward this Hore person. Hell, initially I just wanted to give him back his journal. I promised Dad I'd chew on it.

From the couple of ethics and procedural courses I'd taken in college, and by watching primetime cop shows, I figured I wasn't stalking the guy (having never seen him), reckoned I was using public information, and thus, there was no problem. Before I went to bed that night though, I shot off an email to the in-house attorney at the paper. His response was waiting when I logged on in the morning, providing me with (what I assumed) was a cut-and-paste definition: "Stalking is a course of conduct directed at a specific person that involves repeated (two or more occasions) visual or physical proximity, nonconsensual communication, or verbal, written, or implied threats, or a combination thereof, that would cause a reasonable person fear." He closed with, "Don't do that. Regards, B."

He is on salary, and I figured that's why I got the response I did. If he charged by the incremental hour, I'm sure an appointment would have been required, some background research needed, and a follow-up meeting or two. As it was, I saved the email and forgot about it.

I spent the following two days doing basically nothing. Lots of time chatting with my folks and taking a couple of walks around the town square—and there literally is a town square. A patch of grass with an American flag waving atop a tall pole in the center, surrounded by a two lane circle occupied by all of the town's businesses. A one room library (that still had a small collection of VCR tapes), police/fire/EMT station, a post office, *the* bank, a diner complete with flowered curtains and Formica tables and chairs right out of a 1950s TV show, a shared medical/dental office, and a used furniture/clothing shop. Fifteen minutes, round trip.

Three short days after I got there, it was time to head home. We did the goodbye thing and I pointed the rental towards Lambert Field, doing everything in reverse of arrival, heading back to the Pacific

Northwest, great-aunt Janice looking over my shoulder.

Home Again

By late Thursday afternoon, I was home. It was nice getting away for a few days and visiting my folks. But as that diminutive and inquisitive girl reminded us: There's no place like home. I prefer my own bed and, pardon me for saying so, my own toilet.

Bonus points: Amanda was in good spirits. Life is good. Hoping to ride a winner, what did I plan to do Saturday? Yup. Call Bert's. If my new friend Roully was there, I was heading in.

On Friday morning I slept in until nearly nine. After a late start I got myself situated with a cup of coffee and centered myself in front of my computer monitor, staring at it as though it would get up and dance at any moment. My deadline was 7 p.m. and I had nothing. I knew exactly what I would be doing for the next nine hours. Pouring over a weeks' worth of stats, sports news, trades, and scandals trying to create a literary sports mansion out of matchsticks.

A little after 6 p.m., I'd wrapped up what I considered a decent piece about salaries of women athletes compared to their male counterparts, touching on the discrepancies and leaving it open for a follow-up about how women's events don't attract the crowds—and thus the revenue—as do men's events. The type of piece that generates reader feedback, both online and via email, and my boss loves that. Having proofed it, I hit 'send' around 6:30 p.m.

During my time away, I discovered that Amanda had recorded some of our favorite English mystery shows.

Perfect timing.

I looked forward to sharing the evening with her and a big bowl of popcorn, watching a few imaginary sleuths effortlessly solve murders an hour at a time. We whole-heartedly welcome Sherlock, Miss Marple, Hercule Poirot, and a host of others as our living room guests. Sir Arthur Conan Doyle and Dame Agatha Christie are never far away. Life is good.

~

I spent Saturday morning sanding and scraping the desk. It was therapeutic, but by noon I'd had enough. My hands, being as sedentary as my ass, had quickly become sore and stiff. While that was okay with me, as the result would be worth it, I had a side issue to deal with. The desk was becoming a thorn in Ama's side. She wanted things finished as soon as possible. She wanted cars in the garage, not my *junk*.

"You had a desk, why did you buy a desk?" In my mind, I'd answered, "Because I wanted *this* desk," one-hundred times out of a hundred. In the real world, I just listened and nodded.

That afternoon, I called Bert's and asked if Roully was around and was told he was anchored in his usual berth. I asked Bert to let him know I was on my way over and would spot him a drink, figuring that would nail him to his seat until I got there.

True to form, he was there, sitting at his customary table. I was curious if it was generally regarded as *his* table or if there was continual luck involved. I also wondered what he would do if someone was occupying said table upon his entrance.

He wasted no time waving over the bartender and issuing his order for a single malt (I sensed an emerging pattern). He cut to the quick.

"Mister, you're wasting your time. You're looking for something that's just not there. Hore was an asshole. Plain and simple." He thanked me for the drink. An assumption. Another emerging pattern. He continued, "There ain't no boogey man and there ain't no saint hiding in the weeds. Just an asshole. If you're looking to save someone from themselves and earn your wings—keep looking. You're wasting your time with that one."

"Hold on a second, Roully. You say he *was* an asshole. Past-tense. Is he dead?"

He was just starting to sip his drink and paused with the glass chin high, seemed to think it over and said, "I don't know what to tell you, son. He's in and out of places and lives so often that I never know if he's dead or alive unless I see him, but I ain't seen him for a bit."

"When was the last time you saw him?"

He was slow to answer (keep them drinks coming). After a sip of Scotch he said that he last saw Hore in church, which I found hard to believe.

"It was windy and blowing rain like a horse bouncing piss off a smooth, flat rock. We was both just meandering around town. The church doors was open and it was warmer and dryer so we took a seat in the back row and stayed a bit."

A quick pull on his Scotch and he continued. "We sat there for a while not saying nothing to nobody. Well, Hore starts claiming he was seeing things and then sure enough I caught it too." He peered over his glass at me to see if I was following.

"We thought maybe one of us stepped on a baby Jesus or maybe there was a little something extra in the whisky we shared. Either way, those were some good times."

"Whisky?" I asked. "In church?"

"No, no," he said. "This here was before church started. We wasn't drinking during the preachin'."

Somehow I was meant to believe drinking before morning mass was better than drinking *during* mass. The best I could muster was, "Hum."

"Why not?" Roully continued as if I were dense. "Catholics been doing it for generations. Why, taking communion is no different than drinking a shot. The way I figure, me or Hore shoulda been in charge. You give him a jug of wine and a box of crackers, he'd have people lined up around the block."

Church hypocrisy was not lost on him. To him, that a person would take a knee, eat a cracker, and suck on a bit of faux-wine (all in the name of Jesus), then leave church and bitch about the parking lot traffic was worth watching in its own right.

He began to pantomime, pretending he was driving a car. "Praise Jesus. He is our salvation. Wait! What the hell is that idiot trying to do? Can't he see the signs? Left turn only, damn it!"

He followed this with another sip of Scotch. "See you at bible study Tuesday night, Bill." Looking around and whispering, "Jesus Christ we'll never get out of this frigging place."

Now, I confess to being a little caught up in his tale and went on a colloquy of my own around Roully's way of thinking. About how *the* church solves the world's problems. See, I don't believe Christianity owns this mindset. Everyone's church is *the* church. At the end of the day, those with a religious tilt roll the dice and proactively pray that they land on the jackpot of the gods—finding the one, true creator promising nirvana, everlasting life, or new school clothes. Religions profess that theirs is *the only true path* to everlasting life (in some form or another) and if you don't play along, bad things happen.

Sects, factions, and cults abound. If you have a doctrine, you'll find followers. The more inspired and creative the story, the more believability is suspended and, therefore it must be true. What is the definition of a cult, anyway? I'm going to go out on a limb and say that the definition applies to people that have a different belief than yours.

~

Still there? Good, because all this reminds me of another original friend: Pike. I met this self-declared man of God when I was volunteering at a local mission a few years back. Pike was proud to call himself a hillbilly and loved sharing that bit of information with anyone who would listen. Until his appearance in urban Salem, I got the impression that he had never driven on a paved road except perhaps to get across it. He looked every bit the part of a hard-timed down-and-outer who probably couldn't have recalled the last time he cashed a check with a comma in it. That he was a dreamer was not in question. Pike was always looking to be recognized as the best at something. Anything. It's as though he scoured tattered copies of *The Guinness Book of World Records* searching for a way to get his name in print. Immortalized until the next edition.

Pike liked his bourbon. Not good bourbon, mind you. I offered to buy him breakfast one day and he told me to meet him at The Breakers. Sounded like a nice enough place, but turned out to be a bar that just happened to serve breakfast. Surprise. Anyway, he offered to buy a shot, and I took him up on it (knowing full-well I'd hear about it when I got home). Taking a sip, it felt like someone tossed a road flare down my throat.

I last saw Pike in late October when I spotted him sitting in a diner as I was out doing errands. I stopped in to say hello, and wasn't sure if it was the chilly autumn weather or the DTs, but he was shaking like a lap-dog trying to pass an avocado pit. Entertaining but sobering, holding his shot glass and involuntarily hammering out Rimsky-Korsakov's Flight of the Bumblebee on the crusty wood countertop.

Pike did manage to give me some advice that has stuck with me like my hand did on that sticky counter. He said that preachers are relocation specialists. Preaching to help us find our way in this station of life and prepare us for the next. To Pike, sermons were viewed as packing—preparing for the final stop—and he never failed to remind those within earshot that many of them, including yours truly, needed to hold a pretty large yard sale to be ready for that. Well, Pike, you'd be pleased to know that I did manage to unload a few things here and there, but found much I was unwilling to let go of; vices I'd have to price so low to get rid of that I'd just as soon keep.

As a man of God, Pike found that many others at the mission were a bit scared of him. It was as if they thought he had an "in" with the big guy and were afraid he'd damn them, and it'd take hold. He finally confessed that his Jesus magic never really worked on any one. But, he was comfortable with his lot and assured me that his bags were packed for the journey.

I haven't seen Pike since that day. I hope he's doing well and sharing his wisdom with all those in earshot.

Pike should meet Roully, or, for that matter, Hore. I believe they'd all become quick friends. I wouldn't have been surprised to see them on late night TV as I flipped through the high numbers past the Jesus channels. But again, I've led us astray ...

~

Roully is a talker, but you could never be sure which way the truth or bullshit meter arrow was pointing. He is never afraid to say what he thinks, even when he didn't have a clue what he was talking about. Oddly, I appreciated it. He is opinionated and brusque and straight-forward. You never had to guess where he stood on things—facts sometimes be damned. You take the bad with the good. Frankly, I'd rather someone be open and honest, regardless of their knowledge level on any given subject, than I would someone who sits in the corner of a room, says nothing, smirks at every comment, and wears an elitist halo—regardless of *their* knowledge level on any given subject.

Roully had drained his Scotch and asked if I'd like another beer. I told him I needed to get going but would be happy to buy another for him if he wanted. I'd barely put the period on that sentence before he was holding his glass up towards the bartender like a smart kid in grade school begging to answer the teacher's question. I paid the tab and told him I realized that he thought I should just let it drop, but, as soon as I said I'd like to chat with him some more, we made "bar plans" to meet sometime early in the week. I reckoned that *bar plans* is just another way of saying, "You know where to find me." He said he'd look forward to it, asked me my name again, and added that perhaps we could have a cigar some time. I nodded my head, smiled, and headed out.

~

The next day, Ama and I spent the morning over coffee, crossword puzzles, and general chitchat. Of course being Sunday also meant that there was serious gardening to do. I played in the yard, puttered around, and did my best to look useful and engaged. To be fair, it provided some much needed bonding time. We chatted our way through the weeds and garden. School was going well, work was still frustrating, and she was looking toward the future. Except for the school thing, I was basically a "ditto" in the conversation. But agreement always works. Right up there with hearing our own name, "me too," is a universal symbol of "I like you."

We spent the evening watching an old Cary Grant film and munching popcorn. The sound of which (popcorn, not Cary's mid-Atlantic accent) isn't as annoying as it is in a theatre with someone directly behind you grabbing a fistful and gnawing on it, mouth agape, simultaneously telling a seatmate the plot, describing the sets, scenery, clothes, and generally doing a poor rendition of *Mystery Science Theatre* for two hours.

At any rate, it was a pleasant respite from school, cramming, and work for Amanda and an escape from the world of sports for me. (Escaping sports isn't something many of my readers can relate to. Thankfully so.) While we cling to our movie nights, we approach them from different angles. Though Ama and I share many things in common, we have enough differences to keep it interesting. Soon after we first met, I asked her if she liked movies, and she responded (straight-faced), "Yes, the good ones." And that was how our movie nights started. Looking for the good ones.

We agree on well-acted, entertaining films. And popcorn. Gotta have popcorn. Problem is, however, I am happy tossing a bag in the microwave whereas she'll opt to make popcorn in an actual popcorn machine because, to her, it tastes better. I'll grab a beer from the fridge and she'll make herself something to drink—coffee, tea, a voodoo vinegar concoction, or water. I flop back in my recliner with my feet in the air, big toes carefully framing the TV as usual, while Amanda will, as likely, be sitting straight up on the edge of a chair. But, it's movie night. She enjoys them, I enjoy them, and everything else is a matter of accommodation.

Roully Redux

As long as I was buying, Roully was a wealth of information. How much of it was true, I wasn't sure, but he offered up tidbits by the bushel for me to pick and sort through. I decided this might be my opportunity for the book I'd promised to Amanda and myself and most everyone else who would listen, that I would someday write. Of course, the genre, topic, character, and purpose had always eluded me. But, if I could find it right here under my nose—well then, that right there would be a jackpot. I figured if I jotted down all these tales Roully shared, I might have something to build on, and a great title to boot: *Roullyisms*.

Thinking about what Roully and Bert had said, I felt I should just toss the journal on the bar and say, "Screw it, here it is." I'm sure that they'd just flip it into the trash. Probably the reason I couldn't. It wasn't much, but it was a man's notes—his voice. I'm a writer and like to think that people wouldn't just toss my life notes away. That somewhere along the line, someone would be interested. That someone would care. But, I guess that's just the way the story goes. Everyone wants to be remembered for something or by someone. Of course, my primary goal was Hore and whoever Hore was or is, but I knew that Roully, if he knew Hore at all, would milk the parables over time, just as I decided I would about him. So, we leveled the playing field with neither of us (or, more probable, both of us) the wiser.

Now, when I say that Roully knew how to keep his drinks flowing, I'm not kidding. He could flush a twenty dollar bill from someone's wallet with the skill of a springer spaniel on the heels of a ring neck pheasant.

I once asked him if he'd ever been to Vegas. He said that would be a very, very bad idea.

"Because of all the temptations?"

"No," he said. "Because casinos have home field advantage. It costs a hell of a lot more to get there, stay there, eat there, and gamble there than it does for them to sit around on their asses thumbing a deck of cards, waiting for me to toss my wallet at them. I ain't the shiniest fork in the drawer, but I eat. Momma didn't raise no idjuts."

I couldn't find a flaw in his argument and it helped me realize why I'd been buying the drinks. No amateur, he recognized a newbie when he saw one. House odds were in his favor. He knew how to keep enough interest going to keep the drinks flowing. It was up to me to parse and vet his ramblings. The longer I hung around him though, the more I realized that the truth wasn't my primary point of visiting.

Like going to a casino, yes, you want to win, but you stay even as you lose. Just for the experience. I'd become comfortable with Roully, at ease walking into Bert's, and greatly enjoying my escape from life, as it were. I'd never understood how guys just steered into their favorite local haunt before. But now I get it. It's akin to the theme song from the TV series, *Cheers* ... "*where everybody knows your name.*" Like going home without the expectations.

~

The next time I saw Roully, I was still chewing on his story about how he and Hore had gone to church. I was going to bring it up again, but he'd already moved on. Roully did offer that Hore was a far cry from a prophet, but probably no more so than Joseph Smith, who, as Roully puts it, "was just a regular fella until he got all tanked up and found the goose that laid his golden egg."

Roully saved his deepest opinions for describing Hore's approach to relationships. He rambled, and, indeed it was a little complex, but all the more interesting. He opined that Hore never roped the concept of maintaining a monogamous, nurturing relationship; comparing his interest in the fairer sex to gardening. Well, that's me paraphrasing. Roully was a bit more colorful. In hindsight, I did remember reading something about gardening in the journal and made a mental note to look it up when I got home.

"Gardening seems to be an odd parallel for females," I said. "How did he come to that conclusion?" I asked, and was not disappointed. Roully took a sip of the now expected single malt and climbed his proverbial soap box.

"Well, he told me that gardening starts with fixin' dirt, before you plant seeds and long before you can reap what you sow." He paused to make certain I had an appropriate rapt posture before continuing. "The weeding, feeding, watering, tending, and such. They all come after. Week after week. He knew some of his effort could fall prey to other animals; birds and vultures and other critters will swoop in and grab their share, and some just won't play out."

It was quite the story but I confessed I wasn't making the connection.

"You see," he continued, "Hore, he just cut out all the hubabalou. He didn't want no garden, only the crops. He seen bars like they was grocery stores. He'd save his money, visit the market, grab what he wanted, pay the bill, and go home. All the things you do afterwards, he did upfront."

I told him that seemed farfetched.

"I toll the same thing to Hore."

"Really. What did he say?"

"I told him he was missing out on the love of a good woman."

"And?" I asked.

"He just smiled and said, 'Yeah, but I ett.'"

He looked at me to see if I needed further explanation. I remained quiet. He hadn't moved, so I knew there was more to hear. He bought me a beer (that I paid for) and continued.

"Hore told me he did his gardening on Friday and Saturday nights at a place called the Watering Patch. Wide selection, ripe, firm, some fresher than others, lots of reduced price day old stuff—melons that squish in your fist and others you can bounce a quarter off and a new selection every week."

I listened. His grammar got better, his sentences longer. He was on a roll.

"Told me what he liked, and if he got bored with the merchandise, there was always another market on nearly every corner."

I bit and asked what the watering patch was. And of course, Roully didn't disappoint. Seems the Watering Patch is a bar featuring cheap libations and apparently cheap ... produce.

"One of Hore's problems with the women is he don't love the cats." He chewed on the patch of hair under his lower lip. "Well, maybe not so much that, I guess, but he just couldn't shut the hell up about it. I told him that cats can be really good gardening tools. He liked my thinking, I can tell you that."

He smiled up towards the chugging air purifier and told me that this resulted in Hore getting a subscription to *Feline Lovers* magazine, which he prominently displayed throughout his house and car with nary a cat in sight. "Best goddamn lure ever. $14.99!"

"You mean his apartment or ...?"

"Naw. He had some house out in the middle of Timbuktu. I never been, but he could disappear at times."

I asked if he really thought this gardening nonsense had any value. I got a deer in the headlights response before he started ticking off his list— presumably for my approval. He seemed to be demoting my intellectual absorption rate at a rapid clip.

"Can't speak for him, but let me tell you 'bout me." Counting off on his fingers for emphasis, he said, "There was that truck driver in Montana (*scariest looking woman I ever did kiss on the mouth*), that woman over in the hotel parking lot (*hundred dollar rooms: she didn't have half—and I wasn't running no charity, that's what parking lots is for*), oh, and the plumber (*she brought a bottle of wine. I had the cork screw about half way in before I realized it were a screw-on cap; but good times, good times*)."

And so it went through another scotch.

"If all this is so easy and such a slam dunk, why don't you ever have money?"

He just looked at me and said, "Women ain't cheap. Some is cheaper than others, but ain't none free." He reach out and clapped me on the forearm, adding, "You're married. Best keep that in mind, son."

~

I have spent considerable mental energy trying to untangle the Roully/Hore connection. I've talked with several people and most seem to know little about either man aside from an anecdote or two.

From the journal, listening to folks, and having talked with his daughter, I know that Hore came a generation or more before me. There certainly was no shortage of stories. But those storytellers spoke in respectful tones. It was 'yeah, he was here, he was odd, and he was *unique*.' But no one trashed the guy. The more I asked, the more I wanted to know. And so, here I am.

Roully is a jewel. The closest I've come to this note keeping, obsessive, apparently curmudgeonly guy that I was seeking. Roully was his own kind of man. Self-assured and plain spoken. Not with an educated vernacular, but you always knew where you stood.

The two of us sat in silence as billiard balls collided and people stuffed dollar bills into the jukebox, so we could all enjoy listening to them relive their glory days.

As I've said before, Roully is quite a character, and every time we meet is like receiving an unexpected package in the mail. Exciting, curious, and you can't wait to open it up and discover what's inside. How much is true and how much is to keep the liquor flowing, I'm still not sure. Either way—great tales and I just keep making notes. I had no plans that my notes would surpass the number of pages of the hand-scrawled journal, but, I started writing, and much like Forrest Gump and his running, I haven't stopped. It feels like I'm writing an unauthorized biography of a contemporary man based on second and third hand information (not as though that hasn't been done).

There are interesting people outside the scope of my routine world, and I often find myself wanting to ease into their lives just to see what's on the other side of the fence. For now though, I'll settle for a peek through the knot-hole. Of course sitting around in a bar all day wouldn't exactly pay the bills, and I'm sure my editors wouldn't appreciate the extra editing and massaging that my words would require.

The more time I spent at Bert's, the more I enjoyed it. The place was becoming an easy anchor between errands. Conveniently located, and never ostensibly filled with rowdy people, junkies, or problems. It was a beer mug, a quiet respite with a sign and an open door.

Bert had become a friend and it was an easy steer of the wheel. In my learned opinion, if Amanda hadn't been so absorbed, concentrating on her studies, she'd have noticed and would not have approved. For me though, Bert's was a place of friendlies, not a place to get rip-snorting drunk or cause problems. A place to listen, to reflect, and to consider things in life I'd only written about. Sure, I could bitch that the Seahawks choked in Super Bowl XLIX, but it didn't really become real until being around people who felt that sports are one of the most important things in life.

I was an outsider completely at home. And speaking of, it was time to head in that direction. I paid the tab, made excuses, found my truck, plopped into the seat and pointed her towards home. Amanda was waiting and she had questions. A lot of questions. I smelled of the answers.

Amanda's Doubts

Amanda strolled into my office and picked up the notes I'd jotted about the journal and my conversations with Roully. After flipping through a few pages, she dropped her hands to her sides, exhaled as only she can, and said, "If you think you're going to get rich by writing a book about this guy, you better memorize the location of the 'hold the pickles' button on the register, because you're going to be using it." Another slow exhale. "A lot."

"Look," I said, "this isn't about you, and it's not about money." I hesitated a moment, but before she could resume reminding me of my folly, I said, "There's a story here and I want to tell it. It may be meaningless to you. It may be meaningless to everyone," I said waving my hands in the air as though I was tearing up a losing ticket at the track. "But not me. I'm doing this for *me*."

"Then why don't you go down to that bar of yours and tell the story to all your *new* friends? I'm sure they would find it simply fascinating."

This was going nowhere and I knew from experience it would only escalate if one of us didn't pull the plug.

"Fine," I said. "Maybe I'll do just that. Maybe I'll do *exactly* that."

With that, she marched out of my office leaving me at the desk and in a dark mood. *How about a little support? Or at least some understanding?* Then again she's wrapped up in Amanda's World that, to me, seems to be growing all the time. Now, don't get me wrong, I have my place in that world, albeit a place she doesn't visit as often as she once did. Kind of like a child that gets a puppy and after a while doesn't walk it or feed it, waiting for Mom or Dad to pick up the pieces.

Now, I'm not saying that our relationship is in trouble or comparing myself to a dog. With the pressures of school and her job, she finds anything not one-hundred percent focused on a beneficial goal to be a time waster. And, this journal—my obsession (for lack of a better word), my folly—fit snuggly into her definition of a time waster. She was stressed. A perfectionist settling only for straight A's, a perfect home, and no gray areas in-between. A mental game of Jenga.

Couples flow into roles and come to agreement about who will do what until, over time, it becomes an expectation. Amanda and I are no different. We never had a formal sit-down, write-it-down, work-it-out session. We just kind of oozed into the cracks and crevices and filled the voids. She's always been punctual and demanding—the General if you will. I've always been a productive, dependable foot soldier with a little Beetle Baily and G.I. Joe in me, depending on my mood and her attitude. It works for us. Yes, she gets pissed when I do something outside of her orbit and I get frustrated always being in her orbit. In my (unasked) opinion, my newfound "Hore hobby" is helping us both. She doesn't see it that way. Yet. She'll ooze into it and I'll slowly fill a bigger room in her world again. Giving each other space and opportunity is always a win-win.

On the other hand, I *have* fantasized about a way of massaging Amanda to agree to my little whims. Though I haven't had the guts to try it yet, my idea is to toss in some key words and phrases while telling her what I am up to. My premise is this: If you want someone to acquiesce, sprinkle in some phrases that spark their interest. Say, as example, you want to go to your neighborhood sports bar and watch a football game. It might go like this: "The guys and I are going out for a few beers and *(Nordstrom is having a huge sale)*. I might be home late but don't wait up *(because the sale ends tomorrow)*. There might be a few *(I love your Mom and friends so much)* ladies there, but don't worry. I love you."

As I said, I haven't worked up the spuds to try this myself. If Amanda caught on to that, she'd be on me like a squirrel monkey. I would've had better luck with this earlier in our relationship. Neither of us have gotten older by being stupid. If you do try it, and it works—you're welcome. If you try it and it doesn't work: No, my sofa is not available.

Again I've digressed. Patience mucho appreciated.

~

I opened a fresh notebook and wrote 'what I know,' underlined it and started making my list. A short list:

- Hore keeps at least one journal
- He made notes about friends and things he needed to do and people who owed him money or vice versa
- He once owned a home in Sublimity
- His daughter sold the home
- He's known to hang out at local haunts in Salem

Reading through the items, I could see Amanda's point. It wasn't particularly interesting and it wasn't solving any of the world's great problems. In fact, it didn't present any problems at all except to yours truly, wondering about this unknown guy and also wondering to myself why I was wondering about him. I closed the notebook and prepared for another movie night.

I look forward to these for a couple reasons. First, we both love old black and white films and that's our go-to. Easy to get lost in and second, there's usually no plot so deep that I can't nod off and come back in time to hear Gloria Swanson say, *"All right, Mr. DeMille, I'm ready for my close-up."* The only downside is we typically kick-off movie night by watching Jeopardy. Now, I love Jeopardy. It's just that, thanks to Jeopardy, I don't have to leave home to feel stupid. I anxiously await the categories hoping for something to do with sports or old pop music. What I typically get are categories about hieroglyphics or rivers of one of the 'stan' countries. On those rare occasions I get a few sports questions, I do my best living room end zone dance. The rest of the time, I just sit and brood, listening to Ama rattle off answers. Time to forget about the journal for a while and enjoy some downtime. Nothing to be solved tonight.

~

The next day I made an impromptu visit to Bert's, hoping to catch the eponymous owner for a quick conversation. He was holding court behind the bar, so I waited for an opening then gave the raised eyebrows, head nod.

After pleasantries, I asked, "Bert, what's the real story on Roully? I've spent a lot of time with him, and he is, without question, quality entertainment." He didn't respond so I kept rattling along. "I like him okay, and he has a lot of stories. But I'm not sure how much of it's true and how much should be taken with a grain of salt." Still no response—seasoned and honed bar skills.

"He claims to know Hore. Hell, I don't even know his full name. Or Hore's. I'm not even sure that Hore *is* a name. But, as long as I keep throwing cash at the bar, Roully has stories to tell. You tell me you know Hore and you vouch for Roully. Everyone seems to know everyone except the guy who wants to know anyone."

Bert pawed at the bar with his towel. "Hore's a character, Chris. Not a big talker, but when he does, he either doesn't make much sense or is the smartest guy in the room. I never knew much about him before you. He's a quiet one. Tell you true, I've learned more about him from you that I ever have talking with him."

I scratched an invisible bite on the back of my neck. "I shouldn't give a flying donut about some guy I've never met, who owes me nothing, and frankly is beginning to sound a bit odd."

"But I thought that was what you were finding so interesting?"

"Yeah, but I don't even know if I should be talking present tense or past tense." I closed my eyes and rubbed my forehead like I do when my sinus headaches kick in. "His own daughter won't share anything with me, and believe me, she's a piece of work in her own right."

Bert leaned on the bar, his head on a swivel, but listening, so I continued. "Yeah, I'm rambling," I said, tapping on the bar top. "I'm frustrated. Frustrated that I can't make any real headway about some phantom and frustrated at myself for thinking it matters." I was on a roll, and Bert was doing his best film noir bartender impersonation.

"I'm caught up in the whole thing, Bert. Yes, I want to give this journal back to its owner." I thought for a few seconds, and then realized exactly what was going on with me. "But, I'm finding an easy story that keeps me going, that keeps the water flowing, but I haven't figured out how to plug the drain. I guess I just feel like there's something more. Every time I meet someone associated with Hore, it gets more interesting. Hell, Bert, that's how I met you."

Per his manner, Bert listened and I complimented him on being the consummate barkeep and a decent friend. I backed off of my discourse and ordered an adult beverage of local origin. With so many to choose from, it can be intimidating. But for me, it was easy to feign expertise and order by adjective. Hoppy. Deep. Intense. Since Oregon legalized brewpubs in 1985, microbreweries have flourished here, with more than 190 having sprouted up within the state. As of this writing, more than 20% of the beer consumed in Oregon is made in Oregon.

Leaning back on my bar stool, I took a throat-stinging swallow and thought things through. *Why did this matter? Who gives a shit except me?* Maybe that was the point though. *I* give a shit. This is mine. For the first time in ages, I have something *I* want to do. At that moment, on that barstool, in that tavern, I knew, without doubt, I was going to take this little journal to the finish line—whatever that may be.

Bloody Marys

The following afternoon I got an unexpected call from Celia Browne, wanting to meet with me. I agreed, no questions asked, and followed that call up with one to my bud, Alex.

"Alex? Chris. Listen, you remember that little excursion we made to your dreadfully-named motel?"

"Remember? You kidding me? That was one weird trip."

"Well, guess what. She just called and wants to meet with me again. Want to come along?"

"I wouldn't miss it for the world."

"Tell you what, I'll pick you up around ten tomorrow morning. She wants to meet around 10:30 at a diner just off I-5." I wasn't sure if she was embarrassed about the location of our last meeting or if she was going to be in the area—business or pleasure—anyway. Alex and I showed up a few minutes early and grabbed a booth. She arrived around 11:10, just as we were about to give up and leave. I waved her over to our booth and introduced her to Alex.

"Coffee?"

"I'll take a Bloody Mary. They make the best here. From scratch, believe it or not."

"Then a Bloody Mary it is," I said, thinking about what 'from scratch' means when it comes to the drink ingredients.

"Make it two," Alex said.

"Oh, hell. Might as well make it three," I added. I waved the waitress back over and asked her to keep the tab open, ordered the drinks, and turned my attention back to Celia Browne.

"Thanks for meeting me," she said, staring at her hands. "And," she smiled, "for the breakfast."

The assumption that I was buying—and I was—seems to be a recurring theme.

"So, what's on your mind, Celia?"

"I felt bad about how I acted when you came by. I feel I owe you an explanation."

"No explanation needed or required."

"Well, anyway, you caught me at a somewhat emotional time and it just was a little much to handle."

I sat quietly and, to his credit (and my surprise), so did Alex.

"I had just sold the house and was trying to put it all behind me, and then you showed up asking questions."

The waitress brought our drinks, looked around the table at each of us like she was trying to memorize our faces for a future line-up, and then walked away.

"Why?"

"Why, what?" I was caught off guard by her quick response.

"Why did you show up at my room? Why did you hunt me down? What do you want?"

"Whoa. I wasn't hunting you, Celia." This set me back for a second. Alex looked at me, at her, back at me, and then went face down to his Bloody Mary straw. "I wasn't *hunting you down*." Found myself struggling to maintain eye contact. "I was just trying to learn the owner of the notebook or journal or whatever you want to call the damn thing that I found in a desk I bought from the house *you* sold."

"I guess I don't understand *why*. I find shit all the time, but I don't start pretending I'm Sherlock Holmes or Columbo. You know ... Is it a secret journal? Does it have a code? Is it worth millions of dollars? Does it contain a treasure map?"

She was on a roll. I wasn't going to interrupt, and Alex had effectively oozed into the cracks of the seat cushions, staring directly into his drink.

"Why couldn't you just leave well enough alone? Just leave *me* alone? The house is sold. It's not mine. That effing journal is not mine. None of this is mine."

"So, tell me again, why did you want to meet today?"

"I just wanted to clear all this up. This isn't the way I wanted this to go. It just brought back memories best left in the past."

I remembered the rules about the first person who talks loses, and the best offense is a good set of ears. So I waited, sipping my Bloody Mary. True to the odds, Celia eventually continued.

"My father was rarely around. When that skip-tracer showed up at my door, I figured I was in trouble for something. Come to learn, my dad had passed away and an attorney had hired them to find me. That's how I discovered I was the owner of that place in Sublimity. I wanted nothing to do with it, and the first thing I thought was to get rid of it. It was like closing the chapter on *his* life and another on that part of *my* life."

"So, is that your father's journal I found?"

"How would I know? Whose name is on it?"

"None. But following the leads and such, I've found a few folks who say it belongs to someone named Hore."

"Well, isn't that a coincidence."

I avoided eye contact and again waited her out.

"My father's name was Horace, so maybe his cronies called him that. I don't know." She took a nibble of celery and slid the stalk back into her glass. "He was a watch repairman and clock maker back in the day. I understand that takes a lot of patience—not a characteristic I remember him for. He was always somewhere else. Then he was gone altogether. Somewhere along the line I heard that he'd remarried and had another kid. Also heard that he was the one left behind that go round. Apparently the wife passed away relatively early on. *The Big C* as John Wayne would say. Dad bailed on his kid—oh gee, doesn't that sound familiar—and I heard she went to live with the Mom's sister." She sucked in a straw-full of Bloody Mary.

"Sounds like your Dad—"

"Don't call him my Dad. He is a lot of things, but Dad, isn't one of them." After a moment, she added, "You know what I've always thought was ironic? His middle name is Valentine. Fucking hilarious. Horace Valentine. Sounds like a frigging priest or prime minister or president. Ha."

"Horace Valentine Browne. Not such a bad name."

"Oh, no. Browne is my married name from years back. His name is Chandler." Making air quotes she added, "Horace *Valentine* Chandler."

It took me a moment to piece things together, then it hit me like a wave off Oahu's North Shore. "Aw, Jesus."

"What?" Alex asked.

"Nothing. Nothing. Just thinking about some things I need to take care of." I took a gulp of Bloody Mary and looked at Celia. "Can we give you a lift anywhere?"

"Uh, no. No, I, uh … I have a car," she said nodding towards the parking lot. "Are you okay? I was hoping we could talk this thing out."

"I really need to scoot, but I have a feeling we'll talk again soon. May I call you?" Celia looked to me a bit confused, but that was the best I could muster.

"Of course," she said. "You've been decent enough."

I thought for a second and said, "I have an idea. Would you be interested in meeting at a place in Salem? Very relaxed, and the drinks are on me."

"I dunno. How about you just give me a call and we'll work it out." She drained her Bloody Mary and said, "I thought you were married."

It took me a few seconds before I grasped her meaning. "Oh, I am married. In fact, I'm thinking of bringing my wife along if you don't mind. Just to keep you comfortable."

At this, Alex chimed in. "Wait! Free drinks? I'm in." Christ. I rolled my eyes and told him we would talk about it. I tossed a twenty on the table, stood, and headed for the door.

On the way out to the truck, Alex asked, "So what the hell was that all about?"

"What was what about?"

"The sudden need to leave like you saw the bat signal or something."

"Nothing. I just have shit to do, okay?"

"Chris, I'm not an idiot. I saw the lightbulb come on. What's going on up there?" he asked, poking his index finger at my temple.

"Look. I need a little time here, buddy. Give me some space to sort some things through. I'll call you when or if Celia wants to meet. Fair enough?"

We rode in silence, each of us for our own reasons. After I dropped him off, I hit Bert's. He wasn't there. No one I knew was there. I sat at the bar, nursed part of an adult beverage, then headed home.

The Drive

On Saturday, I told Amanda I'd like to take her for a little drive. Just to take a break for a bit. She agreed, and we drove around the Keizer area iris gardens before winding back towards a small cemetery near the hop fields just east of the Willamette River. As I steered through the wrought iron gates and drove into the cemetery, I could tell Amanda was doing mental calculations. She knew it wasn't an anniversary, her Mom's birthday, or day of passing. Before she spoke, I said, "Sometimes it's just nice to visit a quiet place where we know there will always be a loved one waiting."

I stopped the truck shy of her Mom's grave, near a cluster of rhododendrons and azaleas, surrounded by mature, proud maples. We got out, I took Amanda's left arm and hooked it through my right, and we strolled in the quiet, meeting only bees partaking of graveside flower nectar. It was one of those clear, warm days that make living in Oregon worthwhile. Northwesterners refer to these glorious days as "when the mountains are out."

We stood quietly beside her Mom's grave for a few minutes before I turned and walked away, heading back towards the truck. I glanced back just as Amanda was aiming to join me. I gave the palms out "wait" hand gesture and pointed out a marker a few yards from her. She looked at me quizzically and I said, "Just check it out." I slowly walked back to the truck, and climbed in.

I anxiously checked the rear view mirror every fifteen seconds or so. There was a slight sun glare and I shaded my eyes with my right hand and tilted my head. She had found the marker and was kneeling, head on her chest. The sun, through tree branches, cast her penumbra across the grounds in front of her. I could tell by her slow rising and falling body that she was crying. Her left hand rested on her knee while she softly brushed cut grass off the marker with her right. I looked away and sat quietly. She'd be joining me soon, and she'd have questions. About a man. About a journey. About loss. About a journal.

Ama and I rode home in silence. Once there, I went to my office and found the timeworn journal, wrote "Horace Valentine Chandler" on the cover, then quietly walked into the guest room and over to Amanda's seldom-used corner desk. I opened the lower left drawer, and gently slid in the journal.

Epilogue

The following Saturday, Ama and I took a drive into Salem. I told her it would be nice to share a bit of downtime. She was fairly quiet, remembering our last weekend drive, and still digesting last week's personal tsunami. She didn't ask where we were going and I didn't offer.

Once in town, I navigated the few lefts and rights and slid into a parking spot close to Alvareza's. She looked at me curiously. I shrugged and said, "Come on, I'm hungry." We grabbed a couple of Carne Asada tacos. She commented that there was no place to sit and I grabbed her elbow and led her next door.

Alex was sitting at the bar, and Roully was at his usual table. I went over and asked if we could join him, and he gave me the dog with tilted head, *"who is this"* look, before nodding agreeably. I pulled out a chair for Amanda, headed to the bar, grabbed Alex, ordered two beers and a scotch (I'm trainable), asked Bert if he had time to visit for a few minutes, then hurried back to the table lest Roully scare Amanda away.

As Bert was heading over, I got up and scooted another table together for us. Just about then, as if on cue, Celia Browne walked in. I was a bit surprised, but decidedly happy that she accepted the invitation. I'd called her earlier in the week, but provided few details, as I was afraid she'd run. She was skeptical, but told me she'd think about it. Now, here she was. Still skeptical, but here. I waved her over and ordered a Bloody Mary.

We all sat around staring at each other for a few moments before I finally spoke up. I'd thought long about how to do this, but in the end I simply introduced Amanda. As my wife. And as Horace's daughter. I presented Celia, her newly-discovered half-sister. After the how, why, when, and jaw gaping, we settled in for a few hours of conversation. Amanda sat at the table with the four of us and had a beer. She listened to a few stories about her dad. She laughed till she cried and cried till she laughed. Even Alex was in a decent mood.

As we were getting ready to leave, Roully reached for the tab and said, "This is on me." I nearly fell over in disbelief. At the door, Bert pulled Amanda and me aside. "You know, this is quite the development." He smiled a big smile, showing teeth I didn't know he had.

"I guess everything for a reason." Looking at Amanda he said, "Young lady, you are always welcome here. And anytime that husband of yours decides to stop in, I hope he'll do the right thing and bring you along."

We didn't talk much on the way back to Keizer. A few blocks from home, though, Amanda reached over, squeezed my right hand and said, "Those are good people. We should visit them again." I smiled and kept driving, for once not stupid enough to say something to ruin the moment.

Sometimes the only proof we have is the truth.

Author's Notes

This book is a work of fiction. Chris, Amanda, Roully, Hore (Horace), Bert, Alex, Celia, Petula, and all other characters are pieces of my imagination. Likewise for The Goat, The Sleep Cheep Six Motel, Bert's Tavern, and Alvareza's. As a side note, the meaning of the name Horace is *timekeeper*, hence my decision to have him be a watch repairman and clock maker.

Salem and Keizer, OR are quite real, as is the peaceful, charming community of Sublimity, OR.

Thank you for sharing time with me.

Happy reading,

Michael

Original cover art by Nancy Beaumont, Edmonds, WA

ABOUT THE AUTHOR

Michael Holbrook has written professionally since 1981. During this time, his award-winning articles, features, and essays have appeared in numerous magazines, newspapers, and professional journals worldwide. His last book, *Dear You,* Live! *Love, Life* was published in 2015, and is available in paperback and e-book, on Amazon.com

An Illinois native, he currently resides in the beautiful Southwestern United States. For more info, visit www.MichaelHolbrook.net